Zococa and the Lady

Flamboyant Mexican bandit Zococa and his mute sidekick Tahoka are hired by Don Pedro Sanchez, the ruler of the mysterious territory of El Sanchez, to escort a valuable and precious cargo – his daughter – safely back to him.

But what seems a simple and profitable task soon turns out to be a perilous journey through Apache land. What makes the journey even more dangerous is the fact that Don Pedro's ruthless sibling is intent on killing her before she reaches the safety of El Sanchez.

It will take every scrap of the bandit's cunning and courage to achieve their goal.

Zococa and the Lady

Roy Patterson

A Black Horse Western

ROBERT HALE

© Roy Patterson 2019
First published in Great Britain 2019

ISBN 978-0-7198-3025-9

The Crowood Press
The Stable Block
Crowood Lane
Ramsbury
Marlborough
Wiltshire SN8 2HR

www.bhwesterns.com

Robert Hale is an imprint
of The Crowood Press

The right of Roy Patterson to be identified as
author of this work has been asserted by him
in accordance with the Copyright, Designs and
Patents Act 1988

To the Memory of my Friend, Clint Walker

Typeset by
Derek Doyle & Associates, Shaw Heath
Printed and bound in Great Britain by
4Bind Ltd, Stevenage, SG1 2XT

PROLOGUE

Rio Concho was a small but noisy settlement of white-washed adobe buildings set in a flurry of rambling red roses. Roses that climbed and clung to every structure within the tiny Mexican village.

As the day finally vanished and was replaced by the hours of darkness, the two riders emerged from the dusty trail which surrounded the remote Rio Concho.

The legendary bandit Zococa and his faithful companion Tahoka, the giant mute Apache warrior, cantered into the lantern-lit streets. In most places the coming of darkness meant that the day had ended, but not for those south of the border. To most of the colourful inhabitants of Mexico, it meant a time to relish being alive. Every evening was a fiesta to be devoured and celebrated.

The merciless burning of the sun did not reign supreme after sundown in Rio Concho. The warmth of the day remained, but no longer challenged the people. Men, women and children suddenly appeared from their homes and started to do what was impossible during the hours of daylight. They started to celebrate the hours of brightly-coloured lanterns with unbridled joy as was their nightly habit.

Suddenly music washed out on to the streets. Scores of tables filled the streets and people bought and sold whatever they wanted. Rio Concho became a busy market before the approaching horsemen as they steered their mounts deeper into the heart of the village.

'This is my type of town, Tahoka,' Zococa smiled like a cat who had suddenly discovered a river of cream. 'We shall eat and drink and maybe find a little love in the arms of willing *señoritas*.'

The stern-faced Apache rolled his eyes as he steered his gelded grey. All the giant warrior had on his mind was food and consuming it.

Zococa and Tahoka slowed their horses, and heard the sound of bugles and guitars washing out from the adobe structures all around them.

Both bandits eased back on their long leathers and stopped their animals outside a *cantina*. The smell of freshly cooked chilli spilled out with the amber lanternlight and washed over the two horsemen.

Tahoka urgently spoke with his hands to his partner.

'*Sí, amigo,*' Zococa smiled. 'We can eat.'

Without a second thought, Zococa dismounted and tied his reins to a hitching pole as his companion sat in his saddle and gazed all around them anxiously.

The famed bandit was surprised by the Indian's hesitation.

'What is wrong, little one?' Zococa asked as he

rested a hand on the back of his pinto stallion. 'What do you hear over the sound of the music?'

Tahoka spoke with his hands frantically.

He told his companion that there were riders following them along the same dusty trail that they had used to reach the remote Rio Concho.

Zococa frowned and pulled the cigar from his lips. He tossed the last two inches of well-chewed cigar at the ground and then looked to where his massive friend was pointing.

'Are you sure, my little elephant?' he asked.

Tahoka nodded firmly.

Zococa had also sensed that they were being followed a few hours before but dismissed it as being his over-active imagination. Now he was convinced that he had been correct all the time. Being wanted dead or alive on both sides of the border had a way of dampening even Zococa's enthusiasm. Yet he refused to allow it to spoil his desire to enjoy himself.

'Come on, Tahoka,' he said encouragingly. 'I will buy you much food to fill that belly of yours. We will just keep our eyes wide open for any bounty hunters who might decide to kill us.'

Tahoka dropped from his mount and secured his long leathers to the hitching pole. He moved around the tails of the horses and then followed the bandit through the beaded curtain into the heart of the *cantina*. Within seconds of entering the aromatic *cantina*, Tahoka had forgotten his concerns and concentrated on the hot range where a heavily-bosomed female was singing as she cooked.

They had been eating for nearly an hour when their attention was drawn to the sound of horses outside the *cantina*. Tahoka kept eating his chilli as Zococa rose to his feet and moved to the opposite side of the *cantina* and rested the palm of his right hand on the brightly painted adobe wall.

The young bandit could hear the sound of jangling spurs and hoofbeats over the music. His eyes narrowed as he stared out into the street illuminated by lanterns. For a moment Zococa saw nothing as the noise grew louder. Then he caught sight of the two horsemen as they rode past the window. Every fibre of his being expected the riders to stop but they did not.

'That is strange,' Zococa muttered under his breath as he watched the riders circle the *cantina*. His fingers curled around his holstered pistol as he listened to the sound of the horsemen travelling around the adobe structure.

The *cantina* was only half full of patrons scattered around its various tables. Zococa strode away from where his partner was seated eating and sat down opposite the beaded curtain. He drew his silver-plated pistol from its hand-tooled holster while watching the swaying beads. It took only a few seconds for the bandit to ensure that his trusty weapon was fully loaded.

Then he heard his pinto stallion snorting out in the street and stared unblinkingly at the entrance. Zococa knew that his precious horse was like a guard dog and always got skittish whenever danger loomed its ugly head.

Two tell-tale shadows passed the front of the *cantina*. The horses were reined in and stopped out of view of anyone within the large eatery. Zococa nursed the six-shooter as he heard the spurs approaching the beaded curtains.

Suddenly a man entered the *cantina*. He held a pair of six-shooters at hip level as his eyes darted around the faces of the various people sat within the large room.

This was nothing new for Zococa. He knew that the hefty price on his wanted poster was a temptation that few hardened bounty hunters could resist.

The bandit leaned back on his chair and rested his pistol on his thigh firmly as he watched the ominous figure enter the *cantina*. The beads rocked back and forth as the man's eyes searched for his chosen prey.

Then he spotted Zococa.

'You look for me, *señor*?' the smiling bandit asked.

The bounty hunter lowered his head and glared at the seated figure before him. A hideous grin crawled across his scarred features as he snorted like a raging bull when faced with the sight of a matador.

'Zococa?' he rasped in a heavy Mexican accent.

The bandit nodded and watched as the guns were swung around and trained upon him. In Zococa's mind, this was a merciless bounty hunter and he had barely a heartbeat left to react.

As the man hauled back on his hammers, Zococa raised his pistol and fanned its gun hammer faster than he had ever done before. Rods of golden death spewed from the pistol's barrel and crossed the vacant space between them, leaving choking clouds of gunsmoke in their wake.

Within seconds Zococa had emptied all of his bullets into the bounty hunter. He watched as the man buckled under the impact of his well-placed bullets.

Both the bounty hunters guns blasted into the sod floor in posthumous response to the far faster bandit's volley.

Before the man toppled forward, his fingers released their grip on the guns and dropped them. The grin was now replaced by a tortured agony that had carved a route across his stunned face when he realized that he was dying. In the fashion of a tall tree after its trunk had just been severed from its roots, he fell.

The bounty hunter landed on his face.

For a moment there was a deathly silence within the *cantina*, but then as though nothing had happened, the interior filled again with the sounds of its patrons resuming their meals.

Zococa stood, sighed and then started to extract the spent casings from the smoking chambers of his pistol as he inspected the remains of the man who had just lost his duel with the infamous bandit.

As he slid fresh bullets into the hot chambers, the sound of a female scream from beyond the cooking range behind him caused the bandit to spin on his heels just in time to see the raised scattergun gripped in the hands of a man in a torn sombrero.

'Now it is your time to die, Zococa,' the second

10

bounty hunter boomed out across the *cantina*.

Both barrels of the lethal weapon suddenly unleashed their fiery venom. Zococa threw himself across the room and hit the wall as a swarm of buckshot peppered the wall.

A large chunk of white-washed wall took the full impact of the shotgun's fury and fell on top of the bandit as he frantically tried to reload his pistol.

Then Zococa heard the sound of jangling spurs. He looked up as the man ejected spent cartridges from his scattergun and replaced them with fresh tubes of buckshot. The room was still echoing to the sound of the massive gun as the bounty hunter jerked his twin-barrelled weapon locking it in readiness.

Zococa's fingers were working feverishly as they attempted to drag bullets from his gunbelt and insert them into his still smoking barrels. Yet the man had crossed the room quickly and was almost above his prostrate target. It seemed that the faster he tried to load his pistol, the more bullets he dropped.

The bounty hunter stopped and raised the scattergun to his shoulder. His finger curled around the trigger of his weapon.

'Goodbye, Zococa,' he spat.

Zococa shook his head. He had failed to reload his pistol and knew that it was pointless continuing to try. Now all he could do was await his fate.

As the young bandit stared up into the face of the man who loomed over him he suddenly heard a thud. The expression on the bounty hunter's face suddenly altered.

11

It suddenly displayed the agony that tore through his body like a bolt of lightning. His hands shook and then dropped the double-barrelled shotgun. It landed at his boots as the massive Apache loomed up from behind the man and grabbed the bounty hunter's twisted face in his large hands.

The sound of the man's neck snapping filled the *cantina.*

Tahoka released his grip and the lifeless man hit the floor heavily. The Apache warrior bent over, pulled his hatchet from the back of the lifeless man and then slid it back into his belt.

Zococa scrambled back to his feet, stepped over the corpse and finally finished loading his pistol. He watched as Tahoka casually sat back down and resumed eating. He was about to speak when another man got up from his table and cautiously walked toward the bandits.

'Are you Zococa?' he nervously asked.

Both Zococa and his Indian comrade looked at the man who had remained seated since their arrival toying with his food. Tahoka spoke to his young friend, but Zococa shook his head.

'No, my little one,' he argued. 'I do not think this man is another bounty hunter. This man looks like a messenger to me by his demeanour.'

Tahoka dipped a chunk of bread in his chilli and resumed devouring his meal as Zococa faced the nervous man.

Zococa eyed the stranger. '*Sí, amigo.* I am the great Zococa and this is my loyal friend Tahoka.'

The man cautiously closed the distance between them and then cleared his throat as his eyes darted between the bodies on the ground near the swaying curtain.

'My master has a job for you,' the man said nervously.

'Who is your master, my trembling one?' the flamboyant bandit enquired as he slid his pistol back into its holster.

'Have you ever heard of the land known as El Sanchez?' the man asked.

Zococa tilted his head. '*Sí, amigo*. It is said to be the most dangerous land in all of Mexico.'

'Don Pedro rules El Sanchez and he has sent me to find you and give you this.' The man handed a sealed letter to the bandit. 'This is a letter which will give you safe passage across El Sanchez. I can tell you that he will pay you well for your services.'

Zococa swiftly broke the seal and extracted the letter from its envelope. He studied it and then looked at the nervous messenger.

'It does not say why he wants to see me, *amigo*,' he noted.

'That you will only discover when you go to El Sanchez, Zococa.' The man bowed and quickly made his exit. As the beaded curtain swayed, the bandit rubbed his chin thoughtfully. 'All I can tell you is that Don Pedro will pay you handsomely if you choose to accept his proposal.'

Zococa glanced at Tahoka who had finally finished his meal and was pushing his plate away from him.

The Apache frowned as he downed a tumbler of wine.

His flamboyant companion sat down beside the muscular Tahoka and patted the warrior on his broad back. Their eyes met and the young bandit pulled his silver cigar case from his pocket before opening it. The thoughtful Zococa slid a slim cigar from the case and placed it between his teeth.

Words of warning flashed from the Apache's huge hands and were watched through the trail of smoke that drifted away from the freshly-lit cigar gripped between Zococa's teeth.

Zococa nodded in agreement with his comrade's concern but was curious that his notoriety had reached the secluded El Sanchez and that he, above all other equally talented men, had been personally chosen to undertake a mission for the mysterious ruler of the remote land.

'You are right to be wary, my little elephant,' Zococa smiled and withdrew the cigar from his lips. 'But Don Pedro needs our help. There is something he needs us to do for him that nobody else can do. We must ride to find out why he has summoned the great Zococa.'

Tahoka rolled his eyes. The giant Apache knew that it was pointless trying to reason with his friend when his ego had been flattered. His massive hand grabbed the wine bottle and he raised it to his lips and finished its contents.

Zococa raised his hand and snapped his fingers to a young waitress. As she walked closer, the bandit noticed that she was frightened by the sight of the two dead bounty hunters near the swaying beaded curtain.

'Another bottle of wine, my pretty one,' Zococa grinned. 'And a room for the night, if you have one. A room with two cots.'

She gave a silent nod and rushed toward the cooking area.

'We shall head for El Sanchez at dawn, *amigo*,' Zococa said as his eyes continued to study the beautiful female. 'First we will get a good night's rest. I have a feeling that we shall need it.'

Zococa did not realize it, but he had never spoken a truer set of words in his entire life. They would require every scrap of luck that the gods, in their wisdom, were willing to lavish upon the intrepid duo. Upon rising from a restful night's sleep in the *cantina*, both men were faced with darkening skies and a growing storm. As they rode away from the fragrant Rio Concho, the wind grew even more savage and merciless. The further they rode toward the famed El Sanchez, the more brutal the gusting winds became. To the superstitious Tahoka, it was a warning of even worse to come if they continued travelling on their current path.

To Zococa it was nothing more than a storm which was whipping sand up into a blinding fury. By mid-morning though, the sun was completely blotted out from those who travelled beneath its fiery orb. An eerie twilight made it appear closer to sundown than

15

the beginning of a new day.

Unlike the anxious Apache, Zococa did not believe in mystical creatures for he had always found that mere men were far more dangerous than anything the paranormal could ever muster. The sandstorm was unnerving, but that was all it was to the confident bandit.

A storm.

Nature did not require the supernatural to aid it. He had seen devastating floods wipe out entire villages. Earthquakes destroy everything in their path in a mere heartbeat. Zococa knew the power that nature could unleash upon the unwary.

He had also witnessed the mindless slaughter some men would bestow upon innocent victims for no better reason than that they could. His taut features glanced around the desolate area they were riding through. If there was death lurking in the storm awaiting fresh victims, Zococa would greet it with his trusty pistol.

For another hour they battled between overhanging cliffs and the raging storm until they noticed that their mounts were steadily climbing a steep ridge. Zococa tightened the drawstring of his sombrero as their horses levelled out.

Then they pulled back on their reins and steadied their trusty mounts. Both men wiped the caked grime from their faces and waited for a break in the blinding sand in order to be able to work out where they actually were.

They knew that they had entered the famed El

Sanchez a couple of hours earlier, but now as the storm increased in severity, they were unsure where they were or how close they were to locating the mysterious Don Pedro.

Zococa was well aware that curiosity is said to have slain many cats, but he also knew that they were reputed to have nine lives.

It seemed good odds to the flamboyant bandit.

Tahoka had led them to this isolated point, but even he was starting to doubt his knowledge of the terrain. The sand, which frustrated any attempt to see through its fast moving wall of granules, kept hitting the intrepid duo like a thousand unseen hornets.

Zococa moved his powerful pinto stallion to the troubled Apache warrior and leaned in so that his words would not be drowned out by the constant howling of the storm.

'We must locate cover, *amigo*,' Zococa yelled out at the top of his voice. 'This storm is at its height and I prefer to let it pass.'

The Apache warrior gripped the reins of his gelded grey firmly and spat the sand from his mouth. He knew that it would get worse before it finally fizzled out.

Tahoka nodded.

Both mounts snorted helplessly as their masters held them in check and vainly tried to see a place where they might locate sanctuary. From their high vantage point, both horsemen looked in every direction trying to gain some idea of where exactly they were.

For what seemed an eternity neither the lumbering Tahoka nor his companion could see anything but the incessant blanket of mocking sand. Then, as if by magic, the sand momentarily cleared and allowed both horsemen to view the landscape before them.

The smaller of the two riders rose up and balanced in his stirrups as he quickly took advantage of the brief moment of clarity.

About two hundred yards ahead of them Zococa spotted a strange natural rock formation which appeared to defy gravity as it hung in mid-air over a patch of ground that the storm could not reach.

Zococa jabbed at the air with a pointing finger.

'Look, Tahoka,' he yelled excitedly. 'We must go there. Come on, my little elephant.'

As the sandstorm returned with even more venomous fury and began to punish both horses and their masters alike, the smaller man sat back down on his ornate saddle and gathered up his long leathers into his hands. Zococa waved his arm at the grim-faced Apache and gave out an excited yelp.

'Follow me, little one.' he encouraged.

Both men tapped their ankles against the flanks of their mounts and hung on to their reins as their horses responded and fought their way through the returning cloud of sand. Nothing could stop the young Mexican as he continued to urge the pinto stallion forward, the lumbering warrior closely following his lead.

Zococa and Tahoka proceeded down into the small valley they had briefly glimpsed toward the gigantic rock formation. The lead rider's large black sombrero, which he had secured tightly under his chin in an attempt to stop it from being torn from his head by the savage storm, resounded to the sound of millions of sand granules peppering its large surface.

Only a Gatling gun could have equalled the sound. Zococa lowered his chin until it touched his chest and rode blindly down the sandy slope. The wind was brutal and treated the large horses beneath their masters' saddles with contempt. Neither the Apache warrior nor his flamboyant comrade had ever experienced anything like this.

The storm showed no sign of abating.

It had no respect for anyone who challenged its might and ventured out during the height of its wrath. It was as though the gods were battling in the heavens and mere mortals could do nothing except suffer in its wake.

Tahoka could barely see the pinto stallion ahead of him as he whipped his loose leathers across the gelding's shoulders and forced the terrified animal to keep trailing the courageous bandit. The howling tempest mocked the travellers with a contempt that only nature can ever muster.

The large pinto stallion galloped across the level ground as though its tail were on fire. But there was no fire, only the incessant peppering of the sandstorm which ceaselessly battered both horsemen and their mounts.

Zococa knew where he had caught sight of the massive rock but could no longer see it. Now he was

riding on pure instinct and hoped that the unimag-
inable power of the wind gusts were not knocking his
mighty stallion too far off course.

'Come on, Tahoka,' he yelled at the top of his
voice. 'We are nearly there.'

Zococa knew that his mute friend could not reply,
but the large Apache could hear better than most.
Since losing the ability to speak, Tahoka's sense of
hearing had improved far beyond most men's ability.

The bandit yelled out again. 'Follow me, little one.'

The horses were spooked by the incessant lashing
of sand as they drew level with one another. Zococa
squinted through almost closed eyes at the expressionless Apache as their horses continued to obey
their masters' commands and drove on through the
wall of choking sand.

'Up ahead is our sanctuary, little elephant.' Zococa
spat out the words in a bid to rid his mouth of the
sand that had accumulated in his throat. 'Soon we
will find a place where the storm has yet to discover.'

Tahoka gripped his reins with his large hands. He
returned his hooded eyes to the strange sight before
them. It was nothing like he had ever experienced
before. The wall of constantly moving sand seemed
like a living creature to the brooding Apache as he
vainly attempted to see the boulders he knew were
somewhere ahead of their charging horses.

Yet no living creatures ever looked anything like
the vision before his sore eyes. Only mythical mon-
sters looked like the ever-changing sand. This was
more like the stories he had heard around campfires

during his youth when elders would make the darkness of night appear even more frightening.

Both horses galloped on.

Neither horseman knew it, but this was no ordinary sandstorm that tormented them. This was the tail end of a far bigger storm that had hit the gulf coast a few days earlier and stubbornly refused to die.

It powerfully twisted its way across the heart of the Mexican landscape. Unknown to either Zococa or his trusty companion, the storm had already claimed the lives of countless innocent people and flattened everything in its path. Now as it continued on across El Sanchez, its murderous power might have been depleted but its temper was no less dangerous.

They continued on into the raging sandstorm and resumed their attempt to find the elusive wall of rocks where they could safely wait for the storm to subside. Both men knew that only when the storm had eased up could they resume their goal and ride on to their ultimate destination.

Many might have turned back in defeat but not the pair of stubborn horsemen. They were on a mission. A mission which many had deemed impossible and probably suicidal, yet they showed no fear as they forged on.

The younger of the pair had never accepted the impossible as anything but a challenge to be beaten. Nothing had ever slowed his pace as he had driven his magnificent pinto stallion ever onward. His mute companion always followed his friend's lead like a faithful hound into any perilous situation.

Most might have taken the easy option and admitted defeat but not the two very different riders as they continued to urge their mounts deeper into the brutal storm. Zococa and Tahoka had never followed the flock like others tended to do. They always went against the tide and knew that the only true failure was death itself. While they lived they would buck against the less brave and boldly forge a path to their ultimate goal.

Whatever the cost.

For Zococa, curiosity was a question he wanted answering.

Why exactly did Don Pedro want his help? This alone burned into the young bandit's craw and he knew that no matter how treacherous the storm became, he would not be able to rest until he had discovered the answer.

They continued to force their faithful mounts on into the belly of the storm. Zococa knew that there must be a very good reason for the ruler of the legendary El Sanchez to send for the assistance of the boastful bandit.

Zococa also knew that there was only one way to discover the reason that he alone had been summoned by Don Pedro and that was to keep riding into the perilous land.

Ignoring their own justifiable doubts as to the sanity of their actions, Zococa and the Apache warrior pressed on.

ONE

It had all started a week earlier in the tranquil domain of Don Pedro Sanchez. El Sanchez was a kingdom within a greater Mexican state that had been gifted by royal decree to the family of Sanchez by the Spanish nobility more than a century before. Although there was no record of the land to be found on maps of the vast area, everyone who travelled across Mexico knew of it.

They knew that Don Pedro, like his ancestors, was a man who ruled in the manner of an ancient tyrant. His word was law. To defy his command was to flirt with death. Don Pedro had an army of *vaqueros* who protected their ruler and maintained the kingdom.

Most bandits avoided this strange place, knowing that Don Pedro Sanchez was not a man to trifle with. He dictated the law as he saw it and ensured that his commands were obeyed. To break any of the laws which Don Pedro had created was to sign your own death warrant. Stories of how he would execute anyone who travelled in his small kingdom had reached the bandits and on the whole they steered clear of his land.

All bandits except the two men who were actively seeking the strange territory. Both the flamboyant Zococa and his trusty friend Tahoka had set a course to deliberately find both Don Pedro and his domain known as El Sanchez. For some strange, unknown reason, they had been summoned by the powerful dictator himself. Most men of their profession would have been wary of the motives behind such a command, but not Zococa.

He regarded it as a compliment. It was an acknowledgement of his prowess as a legendary bandit by someone that most regarded as ancient royalty.

They moved through the blinding sandstorm with dogged determination toward the place where they had spotted the massive boulders a few moments earlier. Zococa considered that they had been gifted a safe passage through El Sanchez by the mysterious man they had met back at Rio Concho in the *cantina*, yet the silent Tahoka was not quite so confident.

Doubts festered in the fertile imagination of the gigantic warrior as he moved his grey gelding beside the powerful pinto stallion. Tahoka knew that many men had tried to snuff out the flames of their candles over the years. The Apache had heard the many stories of the remote El Sanchez and none of them filled his massive form with confidence.

Yet as always he followed the more optimistic Zococa wherever he led. To the fearless Apache it was his duty. Many years earlier Tahoka had been brutally tortured and maimed by his fellow warriors and left to die beneath a merciless sun. He was as good as dead until Zococa had strayed upon him. The gallant bandit had saved his life that day and as far as Tahoka was concerned, he would spend the rest of his days repaying that debt.

The muscular pinto stallion charged against the brutal sandstorm as its master held the long leathers in check. Brief tantalising gaps in the clouds of sand gave both riders a glimpse of the massive rocks they were seeking.

'There, *amigo*,' Zococa pointed.

Tahoka gave a firm nod of his head.

They released their tight hold on their mounts and allowed the animals to race toward the towering granite. The horses reached the shelter of the high embankment and moved around the foot of the ageless stones. The riders drew rein and stopped their faithful mounts.

Finally, after what had seemed like a lifetime, Zococa and the huge Apache had found sanctuary from the tortuous driving sand. Both watched in awe as the storm continued to pass by the natural shelter they had discovered.

'We are safe here, little one,' Zococa said and then laughed out loud. 'The sand cannot get the better of this magnificent mountain.'

Tahoka brushed the storm debris off his rawhide clothing but remained far less confident than his younger companion. The warrior knew that things were never as clear-cut as Zococa thought they were.

He checked his weaponry in readiness to use them at the slightest hint of trouble.

'You worry too much, *amigo*,' Zococa teased the giant Apache.

Tahoka snorted.

They dismounted and led their weary horses close to the wall of granite and then beat the caked sand off their bruised and battered bodies.

As Zococa hit his pants to dislodge the sand with his sombrero, he watched as his silent companion crouched and observed the storm as its venomous fury passed them.

The notorious young bandit rested his hand on the ivory grip of his silver pistol and replaced his sombrero on his head and glanced out from their shelter. Both men and horses were grazed by the incessant sand which had tormented them for hours before locating this refuge. Zococa paced to the side of the Indian.

'I have never known such a sandstorm, *amigo*,' he sighed heavily as his fingers extracted his silver cigar case and opened its lid. He extracted a long black cigar and then returned the case to the jacket pocket over his pounding heart. 'This has not been an easy ride for us.'

Tahoka just nodded as his hooded eyes studied the scene before them. The large Apache could not see anything beyond the fast moving sandstorm. It was a sheer wall of movement that moved like a bag of rattlers. This troubled the Apache as he brooded on whether it had been such a good idea accepting the invitation of the renowned Don Pedro.

Zococa was also concerned but would never admit his doubts to anyone, not even Tahoka. He struck a match on his gun grip and swiftly cupped its flame in his hands and brought it up to the end of the cigar. He sucked in smoke until the wind inevitably blew out the flickering match flame.

'It is as if the gods do not want us to visit Don Pedro, my little one,' Zococa said as he exhaled a line of smoke and watched as it was immediately drawn into the raging storm.

Tahoka rose to his full height. At least twelve inches taller than his Mexican companion, he was a giant by any standard and a very rare example of his tribe. Few Apaches ever reached six feet tall, let alone exceeded it by so much. He faced the young bandit and started to use his hands and fingers to talk.

Zococa read the well-practised sign language and nodded in agreement. He thought about the concerns of the Apache and then looked back at their horses.

'We have no water, my little elephant,' he stated through cigar smoke. 'Our horses cannot take us much further unless they fill their bellies with water.'

Tahoka strode powerfully to their horses and patted his grey before looking to Zococa and nodding. He spoke with his fingers again as Zococa walked to his side and brushed the sand off the head of the stallion. He then pulled a scrap of paper from his saddle-bags and studied it.

'The map that the *vaquero* gave us back in Rio

Concho lacks much detail, Tahoka,' he sighed before pulling the cigar from his mouth and handing it to the Apache brave. 'Before the sandstorm, I knew roughly where we were. Now I have no idea.'

Tahoka gestured with his free hand as he placed the cigar between his teeth. His partner watched the short message and then rested his hands on his saddle.

'You are right, Tahoka,' he admitted. 'We need water but as long as the storm rages, we cannot find it.'

Zococa lifted the fender of his saddle, hooked its stirrup on to the saddle horn and then started to undo the cinch straps.

'We will rest the horses and ourselves until the wind stops and allows us to find out where we are,' the bandit said. 'Only then can we search for water.'

Tahoka gave a firm nod of his head. He started to unsaddle his gelded grey as he sucked cigar smoke into his lungs. The Apache was not happy as he dragged his saddle off the back of his horse and dropped it on to the ground.

He had not thought that the *vaquero* who had been sent by Don Pedro was being honest when he had spoken to Zococa back at Rio Concho. The massive Indian mistrusted everyone apart from the colourful bandit he travelled with.

He watched as Zococa pulled his ornate saddle off the back of the stallion before standing in the bandit's line of sight and speaking with his hands.

Zococa dropped the hefty saddle on the ground

and looked at his pal. A cheerful smile greeted the Apache as the famed outlaw reached out and gently patted Tahoka's cheek.

'Do not give me the headache, little one,' he said impishly as he returned his attention to the storm just beyond their shelter. 'Don Pedro sent for the great Zococa. I do not know why he has done so, but the *vaquero* seemed very insistent that we go to meet with him.'

Tahoka made a few simple hand movements.

'You might be right, little elephant,' Zococa nodded. 'Don Pedro might want to execute the legendary Zococa just like you say, but I doubt it. Even so, I do not think he would hang you as well. You are bigger than most gallows.'

Tahoka raised his arms and closed one eye as if he were holding a repeating rifle. His friend raised his eyebrows and shrugged.

'You are right again, *amigo*,' Zococa admitted. 'I had not thought about a firing squad.'

The Apache rolled his eyes, sat down beside his grey horse and puffed frantically on his cigar as the Mexican rested his knuckles on his hips and stared at the storm. A storm which showed no sign of easing up. He glanced over his shoulder at the anxious Indian.

'Do not fret, Tahoka,' he advised. 'When the storm stops we will find much water.'

Zococa returned his eyes to the wall of solid rock that gave them and their horses a little shelter from the violent storm and wondered how long he and the silent Apache warrior would have to wait.

They were pinned down and he knew it.

The bandit moved between the horses and sat down on the sand. He lifted his sombrero off his head and glanced at Tahoka before lying on the ground.

'Sleep, my little one,' he said as he placed the large brimmed hat over his face. 'Dream of the much money Don Pedro will lavish upon the great Zococa when we eventually reach him.'

Tahoka was about to obey his friend when he heard something that was different from the chilling howls of the raging sandstorm. The gigantic Apache turned his head slowly in search of the strange noise.

Then Tahoka heard another noise behind his broad back.

This time he recognized the sound.

It was the unmistakable noise only gun hammers make when being cocked. He was about to turn when two rifle-toting men appeared out of the sandstorm and joined the bandits in the natural windbreak.

Tahoka vainly attempted to warn his friend but his frantic hand gestures went unseen by Zococa. The Apache lowered his arms and narrowed his hooded eyes as he stared at the two heavily-armed *vaqueros* before him. He tilted his head and looked over his shoulder at the pair of Mexicans behind him.

The four *vaqueros* moved stealthily toward the massive Apache without uttering a word. Tahoka raised his arms as one of the riflemen pulled the Indian's array of weaponry from his holster and beaded belt.

Unable to contain his feverish anger, Tahoka went to leap forward at one of the men when suddenly he felt a wooden rifle stock hit the nape of his neck. A white flash exploded inside the Apache's skull.

Tahoka crashed like a felled tree. The persistent howling of the storm muffled the brutal attack. As his face collided with the sand, the stunned Apache help-lessly watched the four *vaqueros* move ominously toward Zococa.

His gigantic hands clawed at the sand but he was unable to drag his massive torso off the soft ground. As his mind succumbed to the hefty blow from the rifle, Tahoka felt himself spinning into a whirlpool of blackness.

The last thing he saw was the four *vaqueros* looming over his unsuspecting partner with the barrels of their repeating rifles aimed at Zococa's sombrero.

TWO

The four men parted both the horses and closed in on the outstretched bandit. Zococa sensed that someone was close but had no idea that it was a quartet of deadly riflemen. As one of the *vaqueros* kicked his boots he imagined that it was his ornery Apache companion and waved his hands.

'Do not disturb the great Zococa, little one,' he scolded before feeling his boot leather being kicked again. Angered, the bandit pulled his sombrero off his face and sat upright. The sight of the four dust-caked men both surprised and troubled the notorious Zococa.

'This is not good,' he observed. 'In fact, this is very bad. Bad for the great Zococa anyway.'

The *vaqueros* loomed over the seated bandit like a herd of hungry vultures. Each had their index finger curled around the triggers of their rifles.

'Get up,' one of the *vaqueros* snarled. 'And don't go for that pistol.'

Zococa glanced to the side and spotted the mountainous Tahoka laid out on his face. A cold shudder etched his handsome features as he obeyed the instruction and rose to his feet.

'My little elephant had better not be dead, *amigos*,' he said as he placed his large hat on his head and tightened its drawstring under his chin. 'If he is, I will surely kill you all.'

One of the *vaqueros* laughed.

'The little rooster is angry, *amigos*,' he chuckled to his companions. 'He does not seem to realize that we have four rifles aimed at his scrawny hide.'

The three others laughed.

Zococa raised his left hand until it hovered over his holstered pistol. His expression did not alter as his eyes darted between the four men.

'You have made the big error, *amigos*,' he said in a low growl, which only added fuel to their amusement. 'I could kill you all as easily as swatting a fly.'

The gruffest of the four riflemen took a step toward the defiant bandit and tilted his head to study the flamboyant Zococa in more detail.

'We are four and you are just one,' he grinned. 'You will do nothing except die.'

The bandit remained coiled like a spring. He was ready to risk the overwhelming odds and strike out at the four men. He stared straight at the loudest of the riflemen and stopped the *vaquero's* advance.

'I am the great Zococa and I do not die so easily, *amigo*,' he said in a growl that seemed to halt their laughter. 'You have hurt my friend and this I cannot allow to go unpunished.'

The four men backed away from the bandit as they mulled the name they had just heard. Slowly they lowered the barrels of their Winchesters and removed their sombreros respectively.

'You are Zococa?' the leader of the dusty group asked.

'*Sí*, I am,' the colourful bandit replied. 'You have heard of me and my exploits? You have heard of the hundreds of men I have killed?'

All four shrugged behind their large hats and shook their heads.

'No, *señor*. We have been sent to find you and take you to Don Pedro,' one of them replied. 'We just thought you were scum who have travelled here to rob and steal. We get many bad men come to El Sanchez.'

'You do not know me?' Zococa was baffled. 'But I am famous in Mexico and across the border. I am wanted dead and alive in two countries, *amigos*.'

The *vaqueros* glanced at one another. Unlike their leader, none of them had any idea of who Zococa was or what he was famed for.

'We were just told to look out for a stranger,' another of the group added. 'Don Pedro did not know when you would arrive in El Sanchez.'

Zococa marched from the horses and men to where his Apache friend lay on his face. He knelt beside Tahoka and inspected the bleeding gash across the back of his friend's head. His eyes looked back to the nervous *vaqueros*. He angrily shook a fist at them.

'I should kill you all for doing this to little Tahoka,' he hissed at them. 'Were you not told that the great

Zococa always travels with an Apache?'

'No, *señor,*' they said in unison before one took a step toward the bandit. 'We thought you were bad men. It is our job to kill all bad men that travel into Don Pedro's land.'

Zococa felt his eyebrows raise.

'You kill all the people who travel into this land?' he repeated.

All four men grinned and nodded feverishly.

'*Sí, amigo,*' the ugliest said proudly. 'It is our job.'

Zococa shook Tahoka until he roused the Indian from his stupor. The massive Apache opened his eyes, reached back and touched the back of his head. His hooded eyes stared at the scarlet mess on his fingertips and then focused on the face of Zococa. A puzzled expression etched his features before he caught sight of the four *vaqueros.*

Tahoka reached for his gun. The bandit grabbed his hand and shook his head.

'Do not do anything which might upset our friends, Tahoka,' Zococa warned. 'These are men who are paid to kill. They are to take us to Don Pedro.'

The expression on the face of the gigantic Indian went blank as he looked between the four riflemen and the kneeling bandit beside him.

As Zococa helped the Indian back to his feet, Tahoka spoke rapidly with his fingers and hands. Yet the colourful bandit did not answer any of his friend's questions. He simply stepped between the mountainous Apache and the four *vaqueros.*

'You have been sent to guide Zococa to Don Pedro,' he said to the four men. 'Then do that.'

'We shall get our horses,' one of the *vaqueros* said before they all turned and vanished from sight into the raging sandstorm.

Tahoka nursed his aching head and watched as his friend moved to their mounts. The lumbering Indian followed Zococa to where their mounts stood and watched as the bandit saddled both the stallion and the gelded grey.

As Zococa tightened both cinch straps, the confused Apache lifted his reins off the sand and watched as Zococa ducked under the chin of his pinto and swiftly mounted.

Tahoka spoke again with his hands.

Zococa gathered up his long leathers and nodded at his partner. 'Remain calm, little one. I am not sure what is happening myself, but these *vaqueros* are not to be underestimated. Just follow me and keep your weaponry ready.'

The sentence had barely left Zococa's lips when the four *vaqueros* led their horses out of the blinding sandstorm back into the refuge. Both the bandit and the Apache watched as the heavily armed men mounted their horses and steadied the skittish animals.

The ugliest of the *vaqueros* glared at Zococa. An evil grin engulfed his sand-caked features.

'It is lucky for you that Don Pedro summoned you, Zococa,' he chuckled behind an array of tobacco-stained teeth as he toyed with his reins. 'We kill all uninvited travellers.'

Zococa turned his mighty mount and faced the deadly quartet and tightened the drawstring of his sombrero. 'It is no wonder that few people visit the famed El Sanchez.'

Tahoka hauled himself on to the back of the grey and turned the horse to face the four deadly men. His hooded eyes and expressionless face glared at them as he watched Zococa tap his spurs against the flanks of the pinto. The stallion walked slowly toward the *vaqueros*.

'Take us to Don Pedro, *amigos*,' he told them.

The six horsemen steered their mounts out into the still-raging sandstorm. The bandit and his trusty comrade trailed Don Pedro's men deep into the blinding storm, knowing that the *vaqueros* were like homing pigeons. No matter what the elements threw at them, they would find their master.

THREE

The tempestuous storm stopped as swiftly as it had started a few miles from the rocky outcrop. As Zococa and Tahoka trailed the four deadly *vaqueros*, they noticed the land grew lusher the further they travelled into the unknown land. The six horsemen watered their mounts in a crystal-clear brook set in a frame of trees and wondrous plants of every variety and hue.

If paradise existed anywhere on earth, it was here.

Zococa had never seen anything quite as perfect as El Sanchez appeared to be. It was as if the countryside had been created by some great artist. As he and the lumbering Apache filled their canteens with the ice-cold water, the bandit began to understand why Don Pedro guarded it so well.

He did not want to share his perfect home with anyone from the outside world. Zococa had witnessed how droves of men could trample everything beneath their boots when they invaded places in search of gold or other precious things. Usually they would ravage the land and then move on to their next target.

Zococa aided the still dazed Tahoka to mount his gelded grey and then threw himself back on to the pinto stallion. The four *vaqueros* resumed leading the pair of invited guests through the lush landscape. As they steered their horses along a seldom-used trail, Zococa noticed a large craggy mountain. Normally he would not have given the mountain a second glance, but the sight of a fine house perched near its summit drew his curiosity.

The bandit pointed at the house and looked at the lead rider.

'I hope we are not headed up there, *amigo*,' he grinned. 'My horse does not have wings.'

The *vaquero* grunted and then spat at the ground. His eyes tightened as he gripped his saddle horn firmly. His voice hinted at subdued anger as he reluctantly spoke.

'Do not worry, Zococa,' he growled. 'We are not headed there.'

Zococa was curious. 'Who lives there?'

The *vaquero* looked back at both Zococa and Tahoka.

'Don Ricardo lives there,' the *vaquero* spat again as though the mere mention of the man's name was poisonous. 'He is Don Pedro's brother. He is trouble. We stay away from him and his hirelings for he is dangerous.'

Both Tahoka and Zococa glanced at one another and shrugged.

'Dangerous?' the young bandit repeated.

'*Sí, amigo,*' the *vaquero* nodded. 'Don Ricardo wants nothing more than to become the ruler of El Sanchez and he will do anything to achieve his devious goal.'

Zococa wondered if this might be the reason that Don Pedro had summoned him here. He did not care to get involved in the feud which seemingly stood between the siblings.

'Do you know why the great Don Pedro sent for Zococa, *amigo*?' he asked.

All four of the *vaqueros* turned away from the bandit and the Apache and concentrated on the trail they were negotiating. It was obvious to Zococa and his Indian friend that the conversation was over.

The horses were guided over a sun-kissed rise and then started their descent into yet another fertile valley. This one was even more impressive than the one they had just left behind them.

The grandest houses found across the numerous ancient countries of the old world had nothing on the magnificent structure that Zococa and his faithful companion approached. The white-washed building had been built long ago in a virtual paradise of carefully tended trees. No artist could have ever equalled the scenic beauty of the house and its surrounding grounds. The flamboyant bandit was seldom lost for words but as he steered his muscular pinto stallion behind the four *vaqueros* he fell as mute as Tahoka.

There were no words to describe what he was

looking at. In all his travels, Zococa had never seen anything quite so breath-taking as the heart of El Sanchez.

The house had been designed and constructed by the finest artisans in the fashion of the old world. Yet it had somehow managed to not only match the buildings across the vast ocean, but better them.

Zococa held his long leathers in his right hand as they rode down a steep incline and then continued on along an avenue of mature trees. The storm was far behind the six horsemen and the blazing sun cast its warmth down from a blue sky, yet the interlocking tree canopies managed to dampen the afternoon heat from the riders.

Tahoka cast his hooded eyes at his younger friend and frowned as they slowly trotted behind their heavily-armed escorts. This was the heart of the land that belonged by ancient royal decree to the family of Don Pedro Sanchez.

A country within a far larger country. An independent land which few from the outside world had ever set eyes upon. Don Pedro ruled his domain like one of the ancient kings that still dwelled in most of the countries which made up the distant place known simply as Europe.

Zococa, like the majority of his fellow Mexicans, had heard of this place yet had not believed many of the tall tales until this very moment. Mythology was quickly becoming fact and it astounded the bandit.

Now as his eyes darted all around the scented expanse that surrounded them, the youthful bandit knew that it had all been true. This was an oasis in an otherwise desolate territory and yet the flamboyant bandit sensed a danger which he could not explain. Tahoka had been correct in trying to dissuade him from accepting the invitation from Don Pedro.

As the muscular pinto stallion made its way toward the large hacienda, Zococa felt increasingly anxious. None of the *vaqueros* who flanked him and the silent Apache had uttered a word since they had passed below the mountainous fortress belonging to the devious Don Ricardo.

Tahoka glanced toward his companion and secretively spoke with his massive hands. He was even more anxious than the famed bandit.

Zococa read the silent words and nodded at the Apache.

They were in danger and they both knew it. No matter how beautiful the surroundings were to the pair of wanted bandits, it still troubled them.

Both men knew that they were vulnerable in El Sanchez. Unlike all the other places that they had travelled to on either side of the border between Mexico and its northern neighbour, there was nowhere that compared to El Sanchez.

This was a country which lived by its own code. It made and executed its own laws and neither the Apache warrior nor his colourful companion desired falling foul of El Sanchez's notorious wrath.

After the long ride along the avenue, the six horses reached the impressive frontage of the hacienda. The *vaqueros* drew rein first and stopped their mounts about twenty feet from the massive double-doored entrance.

Zococa and his silent pal eased back on their long leathers and stopped between the heavily armed out-riders. As a wisp of dust trailed up into the warm afternoon sun, the large doors opened.

Zococa's eyes darted to the massive doors.

A bead of sweat trailed down from his sombrero and slowly rolled over his defined jaw. He looked at the *vaqueros* and then back to his gigantic friend. It seemed that they all were concentrating on the dark interior beyond the doors in anticipation of Don Pedro.

Zococa returned his attention back to the hacienda and waited like the other horsemen for the grand appearance of the infamous ruler of El Sanchez.

The delay was purely theatrical. It was designed to impress, but the youthful bandit found it amusing.

'The last time I waited this long,' he commented. 'It was to see a most beautiful singer in Mexico City, Tahoka.'

Don Pedro Sanchez suddenly appeared from the shadows of the hacienda interior and stopped between the stained mahogany doors. He appeared far older than Zococa had imagined, yet had lost none of his flair for elegance.

No matador could have matched his highly deco-rated clothing as Don Pedro looked at them with inspecting eyes. He was elegance from a long-forgot-ten time, yet carried it well for a man of his advanced years. Although his hair was as white as snow, his eyes were blacker than coal. He stared at the bandit and the giant Indian with emotionless disdain and gestured with his hand to the *vaqueros.*

Whatever his silent hand movement had instructed, only the four dust-caked riders knew. As they dismounted to obey their master's commands, Don Pedro Sanchez turned on his heels and strode back into the cool of the *hacienda.*

Don Pedro was confident to display his wealth defiantly and that impressed Zococa. He had never seen so much gold and silver thread before, but even so, the elderly ruler of El Sanchez troubled the bandit. Tahoka spoke with his fingers and admitted that he too was anxious.

The *vaqueros* moved to the pair.

'Dismount, *amigos,*' the ugly *vaquero* growled with a cruel grin as he grabbed the pinto stallion's bridle. 'Don Pedro will see you in the great hall of his ancestral home.'

Zococa looked to Tahoka.

'It looks as if we are invited into the hacienda, my little one,' he quipped before throwing his right leg over the mane of the pinto and sliding to the ground. 'Come. We might even get a glass of wine to wash the sand from our mouths.'

Tahoka reluctantly dismounted and walked past the *vaqueros* to the side of his colourful friend. Armed with a holstered six-shooter, a hatchet tucked into his belt and a pair of slim stilettos hidden in the tall sides of his boots, the mighty Apache looked as dangerous as he actually was.

Suddenly both bandits felt rifle barrels jabbed into their backs. Both were knocked toward the open doorway. A fiery rage erupted in the Indian, but Zococa's hand calmed the humourless warrior.

Both men stared into one another's eyes.

'Calm down, little one,' Zococa instructed removing his sombrero. 'This is not the time or place for you to lose your temper. We have to find out what Don Pedro wants of us.'

Tahoka gave a sudden nod of his head. Like an obedient puppy, he followed the bandit into the hacienda. His hooded eyes darted between statues and highly polished furniture as they walked toward a massive set of open doors.

The doors dwarfed even the mountainous Apache and stood at least twenty feet in height. Both bandits were impressed by the hand-crafted doors as they strolled into the hallway.

'Don Pedro must have a lot of very tall visitors, Tahoka,' Zococa grinned as he held the sombrero like a shield across his belly. 'Either that or the carpenters had a very big tree they wished to get rid of.'

Even though amused by Zococa's statement, the lumbering warrior remained expressionless as he strode beside his far shorter friend. The sound of their footsteps echoed around the hallway as Zococa sniffed the familiar aroma of fine Havana smoke.

The scent of expensive tobacco smoke lured the bandits into the room like a colourful fly can tempt even the wiliest of fish towards its hook.

The room was in proportion to the rest of the *hacienda*. It was massive. Shelves reached to the high ceiling and were decorated with expensive ornaments and scores of valuable leather-bound tomes. Luxurious furniture was scattered around the room, but it was something else that caught the eye of the bandit.

Zococa stared at the large carved desk where Don Pedro sat just beyond its decoration. A line of blue smoke trailed up from the end of the cigar gripped between the teeth of Don Pedro and caressed the plastered ceiling.

Yet Don Pedro seemed disinterested in his guests.

The ruler of El Sanchez was staring at one of the many portraits in their gilded frames. Thoughtfully, Don Pedro held his slim fingers together as though in either prayer or deep meditation.

'Come here and sit down,' Don Pedro said without looking to the bandits. 'I am pleased that you accepted my invitation to come to El Sanchez, Zococa. Many men do not have such courage as you have shown.'

Zococa and Tahoka walked to the pair of chairs set about three feet away from the desk. They sat down and watched the strange ruler of this mysterious land as he continued to concentrate on the paintings.

'Why have you summoned the great Zococa, *señor*?' the bandit asked as he rested his sombrero on his knees. 'Tahoka and I are very busy people. We have banks to rob, people to kill and I have many, many beautiful ladies to make love to.'

'My agent told me of the men you both killed in Rio Concho, Zococa,' Don Pedro Sanchez lowered his hands and looked at the smiling bandit across his desk from him. He was a good judge of character and recognized bragging when he heard it. There was something else which Don Pedro admired even more and that was blatant courage. 'Most impressive. I have chosen well in sending for the great Zococa and the equally fearless Tahoka.'

'We are still wondering why you require our services, *señor*,' Zococa said with an abundance of self-confidence. 'It has been a long and difficult ride.'

Don Pedro rested his elbows on his desk and studied the pair before him. He tilted his head.

'I have a thousand *vaqueros* who are the deadliest men in all of Mexico, Zococa,' Don Pedro announced. 'But I have chosen you to do what I do not trust any of them to do.'

'What is that?' Zococa asked as he withdrew his silver cigar case and opened its lid. 'It must be very important if you do not have faith in your own *vaqueros* to achieve this most delicate of tasks.'

Don Pedro looked anxious.

'You should be afraid that the task I wish you to undertake is suicidal, my young friend,' Don Pedro said as he placed the fingertips of both hands together and stared through the smoke of his cigar at the confident bandit. 'So why are you not trembling in your boots?'

Zococa smiled as he placed a long thin cigar between his teeth and then closed the lid of the case.

47

He returned the case to his inside pocket and then extracted a match from his colourful vest.

'The great Don Pedro would not send for Tahoka and myself just to kill us, *señor*,' he reasoned as his thumbnail scratched the match and it burst into flame. 'So there is no reason for us to be afraid.'

Don Pedro placed his cigar in a glass ashtray and studied both men opposite him. The size of Zococa's companion troubled the older man. He also could not understand why the Apache had not uttered a word since they had entered the large room.

'Why does your *amigo* not speak, Zococa?' he asked.

Zococa exhaled a line of smoke at the floor and then fixed his eyes on the elderly Sanchez.

'Tahoka can no longer speak as others do,' he said with a shrug. 'My little elephant had his tongue cut from his mouth by other Apaches. I saved his life and he is forever beholden to me, Don Pedro.'

The massive Apache gave a grunt and gestured with his huge hands as if confirming Zococa's words. His hooded eyes watched the nobleman with intensity.

Don Pedro shifted on his seat awkwardly. For the first time, there was expression etched into the face of the older man. He could not hide the utter horror of the statement. The ruler of El Sanchez diverted his attention to the flamboyant bandit.

'Why would they do that to a fellow Apache?' he asked in a naïve tone.

Zococa inhaled smoke and then blew it at the ceiling.

'Since I saved his life, I have never asked and Tahoka has never revealed the reasons,' he admitted. 'All I know is that they did much harm to my little elephant. His tongue is not all he lost during that tortuous ordeal.'

Beads of sweat trickled down the face of Don Pedro as he listened to the infamous bandit. He could not fathom how anyone could do that and shuddered at the thought.

Don Pedro stood and walked around his desk until he was close to the unusual pair and then filled two glass tumblers with wine from a decanter. He handed the tumblers to the bandits and watched them quench their thirsts.

His admiration for the pair was growing with every intake of breath. He had heard of the many exploits of the duo but now was beginning to understand them a little better than most.

'I imagine that Tahoka is a worthy man to have on your side, Zococa?' he said as they drained their glasses of the red wine.

'*Sí, señor,*' Zococa agreed with a wide grin. 'Tahoka has no equal with his weapons or his bravery. He has saved my life many times as I have his.'

Tahoka placed the empty vessel on the desk and then spoke urgently with his agile hands. Zococa read the silent words and then nodded and looked up at Don Pedro.

'Tahoka wants to know what is it that we can do that your many *vaqueros* cannot do, *señor?*' he stated before returning his empty tumbler to the older

49

man's hands. 'I am also curious as to why you sent for us.'

Don Pedro smiled and then walked toward a large wall of glass windows and stared out at the ornate gardens beyond. He clasped his hands behind his back. Both bandits could see that his hands were shaking. They glanced at one another and then returned their attention to the nobleman.

'It is very difficult for me,' Don Pedro sighed. 'I have not spoken about this to anyone in El Sanchez. You are the first men that I am willing to talk to concerning this very difficult matter.'

Zococa was curious.

'What difficult matter, *señor*?' he asked.

'It is most delicate,' Don Pedro admitted. 'It is also most dangerous. If my enemies get even a whiff of this matter, it could cost me my life and El Sanchez.'

The words were subdued and shaking as they stumbled from the nobleman's lips. He continued to stare out of the large window without turning to face the pair of bandits.

'I have ruled El Sanchez for nearly four decades, Zococa,' he said in a low whisper. 'I have many secrets and should they fall into the hands of my enemies, I would be vulnerable and so would my beloved El Sanchez.'

Neither Zococa nor Tahoka had any knowledge of the political workings of any form of government and knew nothing of how men like Don Pedro could fall victim to long-forgotten acts. All the pair knew for sure was that Don Pedro seemed very troubled.

They rose to their feet. Zococa moved away from the Apache to the window and stood beside the thoughtful man. Holding the brim of his sombrero against his chest, he tilted his head and squinted at Sanchez.

'We are both men of the world, Don Pedro,' he whispered in a comforting tone. 'What is it that Zococa and his mighty *amigo* can do for you? Do not worry if you find it embarrassing, I understand.'

Don Pedro looked at the flamboyant figure and suddenly felt reassured by the bandit's honesty. He patted the shoulder of the bandit and began to talk freely.

'A long time ago I had an affair on a visit to Spain, Zococa,' he admitted. 'This resulted in a young daughter. She has lived her entire life in Spain, but after the death of her mother she has decided to come to the land of her father to meet me for the first time.'

Zococa looked puzzled.

'I do not understand, *amigo*,' he said. 'Surely this is a time to rejoice and not be so glum.'

Don Pedro bit his lower lip and then momentarily cupped his face in his hands. He breathed heavily and then straightened up and composed himself.

'We dwell in very different worlds, my young *amigo*,' he shrugged. 'My life is not as simple as yours.'

'Life is what you make it,' Zococa said bluntly. 'What is the problem and how can Tahoka and I help you?'

Don Pedro knew that men like Zococa lived a far

simpler life than those born with silver spoons in their mouths. He cleared his throat and then attempted to explain the problem he was facing.

'You see, I was married at the time of the affair,' he confessed. 'I provided funds for both my daughter and her mother but was never able to admit the wrongdoing. Even now it is most delicate as I have many enemies in El Sanchez who would like to overthrow me. This would provide them with ammunition in order to rob me of El Sanchez.'

'I have heard that noblemen such as yourself live by a strict unwritten code, Don Pedro,' Zococa ventured. 'Your enemies would somehow use your daughter to blacken your name?'

Don Pedro sighed heavily.

'My illegitimate daughter,' he corrected. 'Men of my station are not allowed to have human weaknesses.'

Zococa raised his eyebrows. 'I take it that your wife is also deceased like your daughter's mother, Don Pedro?'

'Yes, but even so this is a fragile moment that has to be handled with tact and care, Zococa,' Sanchez sighed heavily, as he led the bandit back toward the decanter and refreshed the glasses with the scarlet wine. 'No one within El Sanchez must know of my daughter or her arrival in Mexico. Once she is safely in this hacienda then everything will be different.'

Of all the jobs Zococa had undertaken in his life, this was the first time he had been hired to escort a young female. It seemed quite a simple task yet the bandit knew that nothing was ever that easy. He kept thinking of the enemies that their host had mentioned and wondered who exactly these enemies were.

He looked at Don Pedro long and hard. For the first time since arriving at the hacienda, Zococa was not smiling.

'You wish us to escort your daughter back here, *señor*?' he asked as he was handed another glass of wine. 'It sounds very easy, but I doubt if it is as simple as that.'

'*Sí*, my young friend,' Don Pedro said. 'I have many overly ambitious relatives who desire to take control of El Sanchez and that means I cannot rely on any of my *vaqueros*. My brother wants to rule this land to milk it dry of its many assets. If he gets wind of my daughter's arrival, there is no telling what he will do. You, Tahoka and my daughter are in mortal danger.'

'Are you saying that your brother would kill us?' Zococa looked stunned.

Don Pedro nodded. 'He would try.'

The simple statement chilled Zococa to the bone. He could not fathom such murderous ambition in anyone. It made no sense to him.

He filled his lungs with smoke and then allowed it to filter slowly through his teeth as he pondered the gravity of the task they were about to undertake. He then began to nod as the enormity of the task fully dawned on him.

Don Pedro dipped his long slim fingers into his vest pocket and withdrew a small gold miniature locket. He held it proudly and showed the perfectly painted portrait to the bandits in turn.

'This is my daughter, Isabella,' he said. 'She sent this to me several months ago.'

Zococa smiled as he studied the portrait.

'If she is half as beautiful as this picture,' he sighed, 'Isabella is a very pretty girl.'

The nobleman had heard about the many romantic exploits attributed to Zococa and frowned. His expression seemed to warn the bandit that his precious daughter was one dish that was not on the menu.

'Do not worry, Don Pedro,' he confidently announced. 'The great Zococa and his loyal friend will do everything in our power to bring your precious daughter to you.'

'This is going to be dangerous,' Don Pedro warned. 'My brother has many spies and I fear there is nothing he will not do to achieve his goal. Your lives are at risk.'

Zococa smiled.

'That sounds very exciting, *señor*,' he said as he lifted the tumbler to his lips and took a sip. 'I like a challenge.'

Tahoka pointed at his stomach and then looked at Don Pedro long and hard. Although the elderly Mexican had no knowledge of sign language, he understood what the massive Apache wanted.

'Do not fret, Tahoka,' Don Pedro said. 'My cooks have a wild hog already carved and waiting for you in the dining hall.'

54

The smiling bandits followed the elegant Don Pedro out into the hall and on toward the dining hall. The fragrant scent of the meal filled the Apache's nostrils as Don Pedro opened the massive doors.

As they sat down in anticipation, all thoughts of the daring deed they were about to undertake vanished from the bandit's minds.

It would return to their collective minds when they had consumed the lavish feast.

'Do you have a plan, Zococa?' Don Pedro asked as he cradled a brandy glass in the palms of his hands.

Zococa nodded.

'My plan is simple,' he stated. 'I plan to bring your daughter here safely and I also plan not to be killed.'

'Most sensible,' Don Pedro smiled before adding. 'When you return safely with my beloved daughter, I shall lavish a fortune on you both.'

'*Gracias, señor*,' Zococa smiled.

FOUR

Even in paradise there are said to be serpents that have no other purpose than to mercilessly devour everything they desire in order to rule and control. Since man first developed the ability to reason and put himself above the other animals that litter the vastness of earth, he has scrawled stories of these overly ambitious evildoers. Greed was just one element in the make-up of such beings. Not even the wisest of souls has never been able to fathom exactly what such living evil creatures' true motives are.

Some serpents, like the venomous rattler, are easily identified for what they are. They have no higher motive that the desire to exist and will kill whenever that simple action is threatened. Yet the majority of serpents are in human form and look like everyone else. The only difference is that they have a burning madness buried in the darkest corners of their minds. Greed, envy and a perpetual desire to be better than their rivals are just part of what sets these creatures apart from the majority of their fellow men.

They are far more dangerous than the simple reptilian that slithers across the ground in search of its next meal. These are men who desire something which, in reality, can never be achieved, yet they will continue to destroy everything in their path in a bid to become as great as they consider themselves to be. One such man dwelled high in the very heart of El Sanchez and plotted the demise of his sibling with as much empathy as most give to a fly before swatting it.

High on a mountainside in the very heart of El Sanchez, the impressive villa loomed above the rest of the countryside like an expectant vulture anticipating its next meal. Shrouded in clouds that never drifted far from the rugged spire of rock, the villa loomed ominously above the handsome landscape. The impressive structure watched and waited like its master for its opportunity to strike out at everything below its high vantage point.

This was where Don Ricardo Sanchez lived amongst his hunting trophies and stared down upon the land which he was determined to rule.

The ambitious and half-crazed brother of Don Pedro Sanchez was ten years younger and a hundred times more ruthless than his aging sibling. Since childhood, he wanted to become the ruler of the legendary El Sanchez and as the elder Sanchez had no living children, he imagined that it was only a matter of time before he inherited it. Then whispered rumours began to fester throughout the land, and grew with each telling. Mere suspicions grew into something more substantial. It seemed that Don

Pedro did indeed have a child. A daughter in Spain. At first Don Ricardo Sanchez dismissed the idea as being nothing more than groundless rumours but then his dread became a reality.

Suddenly he could see his lustful hope of ever inheriting the legendary El Sanchez slipping through his fingers. If this daughter of his elderly brother was ever to set foot in El Sanchez, his dream of becoming the country's total ruler was nothing but that.

A pathetic dream.

Don Ricardo had an elaborate spider's web of spies that not only prospered in El Sanchez and beyond, but also held lucrative positions in the royal court of Spain.

Detailed messages began to flood into the hands of the dark-hearted Don Ricardo Sanchez. The news that the daughter of his elder brother was the rightful heir to El Sanchez gnawed at the guts of the younger Sanchez.

For all his life he had patiently waited for Don Pedro to die so that he could become the undisputed *supremo* of El Sanchez, but now that was in jeopardy. Don Ricardo had never imagined that his sibling could have ever fathered a child far away from his Mexican home.

Now he had been informed that not only was this female the rightful heir to El Sanchez, but she had already set sail from Cadiz and was on route to Mexico.

Don Ricardo stared in disbelief at the note he had just received from one of his most reliable Spanish agents. It confirmed his worst fears. He crushed the letter and glanced over his desk at the face of a thick-set man who had just brought the urgent message to his master.

'The letter arrived yesterday, Don Ricardo,' José Manilla said as he moved closer to the angry noble-man. 'It came on a clipper which outran the vessel the lady is sailing upon.'

'She is no lady, José,' Don Ricardo spat ven-omously. 'She is the bastard child of my brother. She is nothing.'

'Our agents have already informed us that the King of Spain has confirmed his approval of her right to be seen as the rightful heir to El Sanchez,' Manilla reminded his enraged master. 'We are helpless to defy the royal decree.'

The eyes of Don Ricardo blazed like fiery orbs as he rose from his chair and stepped away from the desk. After a moment of snorting like a raging bull, he swung on his heels and moved to the window. He stared out from the mountain-top villa at the valley below his unchallenged view and composed himself.

'I spit on this royal decree,' he growled.

Manilla had witnessed the growing anger in his master since the first rumours of there being a daugh-ter had surfaced months earlier. Now as the rumour was turning into a reality, he knew that Don Ricardo had become far more dangerous than he had ever seen him.

'But what can we do?' he asked.

The snake-like eyes darted a glance back at Manilla.

'When is her ship due to arrive, José?' he asked in a venomous growl as he clutched the hilt of a jewel-encrusted sword hanging from his hip. 'When can we expect this illegitimate usurper to set foot on Mexican soil?'

Manilla edged closer to his master.

'I am told that it could be any day, Don Ricardo,' he replied. 'They have had favourable winds since entering the Gulf, *señor.*'

Don Ricardo knew that his long wait to become the ruler of El Sanchez was now in jeopardy. He moved back to his desk and lifted a glass decanter filled with scarlet wine. Pulling its crystal stopper from the decanter's neck, he poured two glasses of wine and pushed one to Manilla. He did not speak as he drank the flavoursome contents.

Then as he refilled his glass, his burning eyes flashed at the *vaquero* before him. He frowned as his unblinking eyes stared at the well-built man.

'How many *vaqueros* do we have, José?' he asked.

'About fifty, *señor,*' Manilla answered as he accepted another glass of wine. 'I can get more if you require them.'

'We do not need more *vaqueros,* José,' he snapped. 'We just need enough to see that this young female never arrives in El Sanchez.'

Manilla nodded in understanding and smiled. 'It is a dangerous journey from the coast to El Sanchez. So many blood-thirsty bandits who would undoubtedly kill this female.'

'Exactly, José,' Don Ricardo grinned. 'This female will have an accident. A fatal accident.'

'I am informed that she travels without protection,' Manilla said as he savoured his wine. 'She has only a plump female chaperone in her company.

Don Ricardo grinned like a cat faced with a bowl of cream and nodded in mutual understanding with his most trusted and loyal *vaquero*.

'The girl seems to be doomed,' he said.

Manilla watched as the unsatisfied nobleman refilled his glass with wine and stared at the stone fireplace. Don Ricardo was a man whose appetite was never satisfied. The *vaquero* knew that he could never have enough, no matter how much fate lavished upon him.

'If that is your desire,' Manilla shrugged, 'then she is doomed.'

There was a stern expression on the face of the nobleman as he paced around his study with his wine glass in his hand. He paused beside the stone fireplace and stared at the unlit logs gathered in readiness for the touch of a flaming match.

'Look at me, José,' he growled as he considered his fate with his usual air of self-pity. 'I am given a paltry pittance by my wealthy brother. Just enough to look regal, but not enough for me to be a threat. If not for my own devices, I'd starve. Now after all these years of waiting like an obedient hunting hound, I am to have my inheritance stolen by my brother's bastard child.'

Manilla followed his master to the fireplace. A sly

grin lit up his face as his fingers searched for a match in his vest pockets. He produced a match and grinned.

'Do you wish me to light the fire, *señor*?' he asked in a way that said so many things that never passed his lips.

Don Ricardo looked at Manilla. The grin was infectious.

'*Sí*. Light the fire, José,' he said threateningly. 'I give you permission to burn all memory of my brother's daughter and erase it from history. I have waited too long to become the ruler of El Sanchez.'

'I understand,' Manilla scratched the match across the stone hearth and touched the papers between the logs. As the flames curled around the wood, the deadly *vaquero* blew the match out and nodded to his master. He returned his sombrero to his greasy black hair and spun on his heels. 'I will make sure that Don Pedro's daughter never reaches El Sanchez.'

Don Ricardo threw his head back and gave a guttural laugh as the *vaquero* exited the room.

'When she is dead,' he hissed like a viper, 'we shall see to it that Don Pedro speedily follows her to the grave. Then El Sanchez will be mine.'

The sound of echoing laughter lingered in the large room as Jose Manilla marched out to dutifully fulfil his master's orders.

FIVE

The land east of the El Sanchez consisted of many dif-
fering terrains, which varied from scenic mountains
and forests to arid deserts. Swamps nestled a mere
stone's throw from the tropical paradise and the trails
were notoriously treacherous for any who dared to
negotiate their meandering routes. Villages were
dotted at various intervals with mostly adobe structures. The pair of determined horsemen had started
out for the distant sea port early and after an hour of
riding the sky lit up as dawn finally arrived.

Zococa and the trusty Tahoka had never travelled
this way before and were unfamiliar with its winding
trail, yet neither slowed their pace. Don Pedro had
instructed them as to the numerous hazards between
El Sanchez and the coast before they had departed
the hacienda, but even his words of warning had not
fully described the strange trail to them.

The mighty pinto stallion strained at its reins as it
fought with its master to start galloping. But anything
faster than a mere trot could prove lethal in this part

of their long journey and Zococa knew it.

Don Pedro had explained that roughly five miles east of El Sanchez the land would appear lush and solid but in truth was anything but. The smooth green land hid a treacherous secret beneath its emerald covering.

Quicksand.

What looked like firm ground was in fact a deadly mire. Nobody knew how many creatures had been consumed by the seemingly stable terrain. Don Pedro had instructed the men to stick to the wide rough trail between countless trees and not to deviate from it at any cost.

Zococa and Tahoka followed the trail methodically and longed to reach the wall of solid granite that Don Pedro had informed them marked the end of the lethal quicksand. Only then could they give their mounts free rein and allow the horses to make up the precious time they were losing as they steered along the trail through the invisible swamp.

'This is a most unusual place,' Zococa quipped as he held his powerful stallion in check. 'The ground to either side of the road looks solid enough. Do you not agree, little one?'

Tahoka shook his head.

'But look at it,' Zococa added. 'I think we could ride across that meadow. Don Pedro is being over-cautious, I think. That ground looks solid enough to me.'

The massive Apache moved his grey gelding level with his young friend and gave a grunt. He then reached up, snapped an overhanging branch and waved it at his colourful friend. He then threw the five-foot-long branch out on to the seemingly firm ground.

The branch hit the green ground and then suddenly sank leaving no trace upon the surface. The smug Apache looked at the open-mouthed Zococa.

'I think we shall stick to the trail, my wise little elephant,' he gulped. 'Do you not think this is wise?'

Tahoka gave a nod.

Mexico was indeed a land of many hidden secrets and like so many others it harboured death in the most unexpected of exotic places. After what had felt like a tortuous lifetime, the riders eventually left the tranquil, but deceivingly deadly, swamp and rode down to a massive wall of rocks.

The riders watered their mounts and then set out again for the coast at increased pace. Both knew that Don Pedro knew this land far better than most and they would follow his verbal guidance to the letter.

The treacherous land behind them was proof that the nobleman was far wiser than his reputation gave him credit for. The pinto galloped along the sturdy ground with the gelded grey close behind its whipping tail.

Zococa narrowed his eyes and stared through the brilliant rays of the rising sun at the dozens of white washed adobes a few miles ahead. The small settlement was exactly where Don Pedro had said it would be.

They thundered on.

The intrepid pair had barely covered a mile from

the deceptive swampland when a volley of ear-splitting sounds seemed to come from every direction. It was like an overture of enraged hornets as the noise echoed off the rocks that towered above their trusty mounts. Then as they drew rein and slowed their horses' pace, both men realized that this was no innocent sound which they had heard.

It was far more lethal than that.

The familiar sound of bullets pinging off the boulders that flanked them suddenly made both horsemen aware that they were being used for target practice.

The mighty pinto reared up and kicked out at the disturbed air as its master hung on and looked all around the rocky canyon walls in a desperate bid to spot their determined attackers.

As the stallion landed heavily on the rough ground, another volley of rifle shots rang out. Bullets flew past the pair of confused horsemen.

They were closer now as their attackers began to home in on their potential targets. Tahoka ducked as one bullet carved a path a few inches from his long plaited mane of hair. The unseen bullet had come so close that the Apache had felt its heat across his face.

He urgently spoke with his hands.

'Do not fret, little one,' Zococa shouted above the deafening din. 'I have a plan. Dismount before run.'

Zococa threw himself from his high-shouldered horse, grabbed its loose leathers and led the black and white animal toward the canyon wall. Tahoka dismounted and dragged his gelded grey after the stallion and then pressed his wide frame against the boulders.

The famed young bandit had worked out by the puffs of smoke discharging from their attackers' rifle barrels that they were all firing from only one side of the canyon. The very side that he and the giant Apache were resting against.

As Zococa pulled his pistol from its holster and checked that it was fully loaded, he glanced up at the troubled warrior beside him.

'You are still fretting, *amigo*,' he said as he stared at the shadows on the canyon floor. 'Do not worry. We are dealing with men who do not seem to be able to use their brains. If you intend to bushwhack someone in a canyon, you should put your rifles on both sides. How can you catch your target in a crossfire from only one side?'

The mute warrior pointed at the shadows. They could see the unmistakable shadows of four men toting rifles as they ran across the top of the boulders above them.

Zococa nodded.

'I see them, little elephant,' he said as he cocked the hammer of his pistol and glanced upward. The overhanging rocks gave the pair perfect cover but it also meant that the bandit could not see a target to aim his trusty six-shooter at.

Then both men heard a rumble above them.

They glanced at one another in confusion.

'What is that?' Zococa gasped in terrified awe.

The words had no sooner left his lips than both he and Tahoka found out exactly what had made the noise.

SIX

The chilling sound increased in its intensity as dusty debris flowed like a waterfall from the top of the canyon wall above the pair of startled bandits. Shielding their precious mounts as countless smaller rocks preceded several massive boulders, both Zococa and Tahoka watched in helpless shock.

The mysterious bushwhackers above them had dislodged the rocks in a futile attempt to fulfil their deadly agenda. As the last of the loose rocks bounced off the weather-hardened sand, Zococa tossed the stallions reins to the gigantic Apache.

'Wait here, little one,' the bandit ordered Tahoka. 'I have something to do.'

Tahoka was still spitting sand when he realized that Zococa had vanished from view. The warrior was uneasy and visibly annoyed. He never liked being abandoned by his younger companion.

Out of sight of the Apache warrior, Zococa ascended the rugged canyon wall with the agility of a mountain goat. Even though the colourful bandit had never had call to climb the side of a rock-face before, Zococa had climbed the sides of countless buildings to many balconies in his quest to make love to numerous señoritas.

The practice had come in useful. Zococa reached the top of the ridge in fast time and pressed his lean frame against the sand as he slid his pistol from its holster. He narrowed his eyes as he squinted against the blinding sun.

Dust floated a few inches above the surface of the sun-baked top of the canyon. Then the bandit spied the men that had not only fired enough lead to fell a grizzly, but had also attempted to flatten Tahoka and himself.

Whoever they were, they did not look like bounty hunters, he thought as he crawled silently over the edge of the jagged rocks and lay facing the quartet of well-armed men.

Zococa's mind raced as he tried to evaluate the ambushers but no matter how hard he tried, he simply could not figure out who or what they were.

Although they resembled Mexican bandits, Zococa did not recognize any of them. Then his mind recalled the words of warning that Don Pedro had spoken shortly before he and Tahoka had left the hacienda at the heart of El Sanchez.

Were these riflemen agents for the dark-hearted Don Ricardo?

There was only one way to discover the truth, Zococa told himself as he slid like a sidewinder toward the four men near the very rim of the canyon edge. He had to get one of these dust-caked men to reveal himself to him.

Zococa kept crawling.

Beneath the unyielding sun, the four riflemen were gathered on the canyon ridge like a flock of expectant vultures. Between them, they had already kicked every loose rock and boulder off the high rim and were searching for others.

Suddenly they stopped.

The sound of Zococa's gun hammer came as an unwelcome surprise as he rose to his feet ten yards to their right. Each of the sombrero-wearing men tilted their heads in turn and stared at the lean bandit.

Zococa held his pistol in his steady left hand.

The bandit grinned as one by one they dropped their repeating rifles without him having to tell them to do so.

'*Gracias, amigos,*' Zococa nodded as he moved slowly toward them. 'Now you have many questions to answer.'

'What if we choose not to answer your stinking questions, pretty boy?' the closest of the four men growled at the bandit as they squared up to Zococa.

Zococa stopped in his tracks and studied the four men carefully. He still did not recognize any of them but noticed that they all hand twin holsters hanging from their gun-belts.

'I am the great Zococa,' he informed them. 'If you have heard of me, you will know that I am the finest shot in all of Mexico.'

They all laughed.

'We have all heard that you claim to be many things, Zococa,' one of the burly men spat. 'The greatest shot, the greatest lover and the finest thief. Nobody is that great, Zococa.'

The flamboyant bandit looked offended.

'But I am truly great, *amigos*,' he protested. 'I have practically filled entire graveyards on my own. My exploits with the ladies is legendary and I have never met a lock or safe that I could not open with a tooth-pick.'

The four men took a stride forward and then rested their hands on the grips of their holstered guns.

'We should kill him and be done with it,' the man at the far right of the line suggested. 'I detest pretty little boys who pretend to be grown men.'

The central figure nodded in agreement.

'He is pitiful when you get a good look at him,' he snorted before projecting a ball of mucus at Zococa. 'Why Don Ricardo wants him dead is a mystery to me.'

The name of Don Pedro's brother caused Zococa to raise an eyebrow as he kept the gleaming gun barrel trained on the four muscular gunmen. His fertile imagination raced as he suddenly realized that the elderly Don Pedro had been correct.

'So you know Don Ricardo, *amigos*?' he smiled.

The expressions on their faces suddenly became confused. They studied the bandit carefully as their trigger fingers twitched in readiness.

'Do you know Don Ricardo?' one asked.

'How do you know him?' another piped up.

Zococa shrugged.

'I do not exactly know him,' he admitted before adding. 'But I know his brother. Don Pedro told me that his brother was the most untrustworthy person in all of El Sanchez.'

'What do you mean, Zococa?' the closest of the hired assassins asked.

'He will not pay you,' Zococa teased the four men as his unblinking eyes watched their hands carefully. If any of them drew their weaponry, he was ready to respond. 'I have been told that if anyone dares to ask for payment, he simply hires someone else to kill them.'

It was like watching four separate volcanoes slowly erupting before him as confusion blended with fury in the quartet of vicious killers. When their tormented minds could no longer deal with the thoughts that Zococa had planted in them, they sprang into action.

All four men dragged their six-shooters from their holsters at almost the same time. Before any of the weapons could be raised, aimed and fired at the slender bandit, Zococa fanned his gun hammer and sprayed them with hot lead.

With smoke billowing from the barrel of his pistol, Zococa started toward them. Three of the men crumpled and fell lifelessly to the ground, but as the young bandit opened the chamber of his six-gun and emptied its spent casings he noticed that one of the ambushers remained upright with both his guns in his hands.

Zococa paused and hastily started to pluck fresh bullets from his gun belt and insert them into the hot chambers. He did not take his eyes off the lumbering man that somehow refused to die. The man summoned every scrap of his dwindling strength and straightened up.

The youthful bandit could easily see a bullet hole in the bushwhacker's chest as it pumped scarlet gore.

'One gun is not enough, Zococa,' he drawled at the bandit who was still trying to reload his pistol. 'Not when faced by so many. It is a lesson you should have learned long ago, but now it is too late for you.'

Zococa felt his heart quicken as both the stricken man's guns were levelled at him. He snapped his smoking chamber back into the body of the pistol as the man pulled hard on his triggers. Two rods of blinding venom spewed from his guns in deafening succession. One bullet tore into the sandy ground a few feet from him whilst the shot from his other six-gun ripped through the dry canyon air and caught the wide brim of Zococa's sombrero. The hat was torn from his head and landed on his back suspended by its drawstring.

'Why do you not die, *señor*?' Zococa asked as he pulled his hammer back with his thumb. But the ambusher refused to succumb to his injury and dragged his own gun hammers back once more.

Zococa watched in horror as both his foe's guns were raised and levelled at him again. The bandit trained his silver pistol at the ominous figure and curled his finger around its hammer.

The man gave out a horrific scream. A scream no siren could have ever emulated in its blood-chilling repulsiveness. Every ounce of colour drained from the ambusher's features and his eyes rolled up into his head. His hands released their grip on the guns, shook violently and then dropped his primed weaponry on to the ground.

Zococa watched in stunned horror as the burly figure abruptly fell forward and crashed headlong into the white sand. The young bandit cautiously edged closer and satisfied himself that all four men were dead. Only then did he holster his pistol again and shake his head.

Zococa bit his lower lip thoughtfully.

'So Don Ricardo is trying to kill the great Zococa and the loyal Tahoka,' he muttered as he circled his prey like an eagle on a warm thermal. 'Don Pedro was right. This means the little lady is in peril as well.'

He withdrew the miniature locket from his vest and studied the tiny portrait. Isabella was indeed a very beautiful young woman and if there was anything that Zococa valued above all else, it was beautiful females.

'You shall not be harmed, pretty lady,' the bandit told the image before kissing the picture and returning it to the safety of his pocket. He then retrieved his sombrero from his back before returning it to his head. 'This I promise.'

Dust kicked up off his heels as the bandit speedily made his way back down to his waiting comrade.

There was renewed urgency in Zococa with the confirmation that Isabella Sanchez was indeed in danger.

Both horsemen spurred hard.

SEVEN

News of the *vaqueros'* deaths spread like wildfire and within hours reached the ears of Don Ricardo Sanchez in his lofty stronghold. The wealthy nobleman paced around his library like a caged mountain lion as he brooded and plotted his next move.

José Manilla stood beside his dust-caked henchman and vividly described the fate of the four men he had sent to ambush the famed Zococa and his trusty Apache companion. Knowing that Don Ricardo did not suffer failure well, Manilla had to embellish every well-chosen word of how Zococa had killed the *vaqueros.*

Finally, Don Ricardo waved his hand and silenced Manilla.

His eyes flashed in anger at Manilla and one of the many men that they had sent in order not only to kill the bandits but lethally prevent Don Pedro's daughter from ever reaching El Sanchez.

The nobleman dismissed the *vaquero* and then sat in a throne-like chair beside his roaring fire. He mumbled under his breath as he watched the dancing flames before him. After what seemed like an eternity to his loyal henchman, he glanced at Manilla and signalled silently for him to sit opposite him.

Manilla did not dare speak. He had seen the dark-hearted nobleman lose his temper far too many times to risk enraging Don Ricardo. Then the silence between the men was shattered into a million pieces as Don Ricardo shouted across the distance between them.

'You said you have fifty *vaqueros*, José,' the wealthy man growled as a plan fermented in his depraved brain. 'Get them.'

Manilla's jaw dropped and left the henchman open-mouthed by his master's demand. He had not expected Don Ricardo to order him to gather up the rest of his infamous *vaqueros* and wondered why the villainous creature sat opposite him wanted them at his high retreat.

'You want all our *vaqueros* here, Don Ricardo?' Manilla repeated the demand.

Don Ricardo abruptly stood.

'I want them here with their horses and fully armed, José,' the venomous Don Ricardo smiled as he traced a thumbnail along his jaw thoughtfully. 'I shall lead them out of El Sanchez myself. We have the most important task to undertake and nothing must hamper us.'

Manilla cautiously rose from his chair. 'Not all our *vaqueros* are close, master. I have dispatched ten of

77

them to head toward the coastal roads. There are three roads that Zococa and the Indian might take after collecting the female. I have each road covered.'

Don Ricardo swiftly calculated how many men were available and then nodded firmly. He strode to his desk and filled a glass tumbler to its brim.

'That leaves roughly thirty-six if you deduct the four *vaqueros* killed by Zococa,' he reasoned before raising the glass and taking a large gulp of the red wine. 'That should be more than enough.'

'*Sí, señor,*' Manilla agreed. 'I can guarantee that each and every one of them is deadly with their weapons.'

Don Ricardo drained the last of his wine and then lowered the tumbler from his lips. His eyes seemed to glow in the firelight as they burned across the room at Manilla.

'We cannot underestimate this Zococa, José,' he warned. 'He has already disposed of four of your best men as if he was swatting flies. Zococa might be far more dangerous than we first assumed.'

Don Ricardo glanced out of the high window for a brief moment. The sun was lower in the sky as it made its daily descent toward the horizon. It was slowly getting darker and the nobleman knew that within the next couple of hours, the merciless orb of gold would vanish for another evening. His smile widened as he returned his attention to his underling.

'It will soon be dark, José.' He repeated his

thoughts and ran his knuckles across his gritted teeth, 'I like the idea of riding after Zococa after sunset. The shadows of night can conceal many things from even the most alert of souls. Even an army. Zococa and his Indian *amigo* will be dead long before they can deliver my niece to Don Pedro.'

Manilla smiled in agreement. He placed his sombrero on his head and tightened its drawstring. He knew that Don Ricardo was perfectly correct about the young bandit.

'I shall send for the rest of our *vaqueros*, master,' Manilla said as he backed away from his brooding employer. 'I shall also have your mount readied. We will be on the coast road within the hour.'

'Excellent.' Don Ricardo emptied the contents of the decanter into his tumbler and lifted it off the desk. He said nothing as Manilla exited the room. Then he sipped the flavoursome wine and smiled to himself. 'I shall enjoy killing both Zococa and his gigantic friend when we catch up with them, but most of all I look forward to destroying my pathetic brother's bastard daughter. El Sanchez will soon be mine.'

The mountainous home resonated with a chilling laughter. It was not a laughter based upon humour, but rather the disturbing cackling that spews from the guts of creatures with demented minds.

Don Ricardo finished his wine and then propelled his glass tumbler at the roaring fire in its stone cradle. A million splinters of shattered crystal fragments lay all around the blazing logs. Tiny shafts of firelight

reflected off each and every one of them as the nobleman stormed out of the room.

He descended the stone steps toward the courtyard.

EIGHT

Mexico was in a constant turmoil as one precarious disaster followed another. There had been so many civil wars over the years that few knew exactly who was and who was not in control of the vast land. Only El Sanchez appeared to remain stable within the otherwise warring country. Yet even El Sanchez was not immune to trouble.

Greed was said to be a green-eyed monster and in many ways this was an understatement to what was fermenting in the otherwise stable land of El Sanchez. For few men had so much greed burning in their innards as Don Ricardo Sanchez. History is littered with those whose ambition destroyed everything in a vain bid to obtain that which was not theirs.

Don Ricardo had mustered every one of his highly paid *vaqueros* to meet him in the courtyard of his mountain home and as his cruel eyes studied the gathering crowd of mercenaries, he suddenly had no doubt as to his motives.

There is nothing worse or more dangerous than knowing that you are right. Even when you are wrong.

The wise never tread this path, but Don Ricardo Sanchez was far from being wise. As with all men cut from a similar cloth as the arrogant Sanchez, he could justify everything he had done, was doing or intended to do.

In his mind, he could do wrong and was always right.

The thought of slaughtering his brother's daughter meant nothing to him. He had told himself many times since learning of her existence, that she simply had to die.

It was the only thing he could do if he ever wanted to inherit the land of El Sanchez. In his mind, it was as simple as that.

Don Ricardo glanced upward at the darkening sky and then returned his attention to the riders who now filled his massive courtyard. He shook his clenched fists at the crowd and relished their cheers.

'This is a holy mission,' he boomed out at the watching horsemen. 'This is a crusade. We have one aim and that is to prevent the land of El Sanchez from being taken from us by an unworthy little girl. You, my loyal *vaqueros*, will enable me to keep El Sanchez. I shall bestow many riches upon you all once we have achieved our goal.'

Then from the stables, José Manilla rode his horse and led his master's white charger through the crowd toward Don Ricardo on the hacienda steps. The *vaqueros* cheered as they watched the arrogant Sanchez mount his white stallion.

Then Don Ricardo gave out a sickening call and led his horsemen out of the courtyard.

The walls of the hacienda echoed to the sound of horses' hoofs as the bloodthirsty riders followed their leader out into the dimming daylight.

NINE

Neither Zococa nor his equally intrepid fellow bandit had rested as night swept across the Mexican countryside. Both knew that they could save untold hours by defying their weariness and forging on toward the coast. El Sanchez supremo Don Pedro had informed them that the ship would not be making for any of the more popular sea ports dotted along the eastern flank of Mexico, but was headed for a far smaller place to drop anchor.

The countryside grew even more dark and threatening as the pair of intrepid bandits lashed the flanks of their powerful mounts. Neither Zococa nor his trusty friend Tahoka had ever ventured this far east before and none of its varied terrain was familiar.

The two horsemen skirted down into a deep valley which was flanked by large rounded boulders. Only the eerie light of the thin sliver of moon lit up the long trail, which they had been informed would lead them straight into the isolated port at which a large vessel was due to tie up.

The shadows were blacker than either rider cared for. In their dubious profession, it did not pay to ride into any place that seemed to have been designed for ambush. Yet that was exactly what they were doing.

The mute Tahoka had ridden a few strides ahead of the powerful pinto stallion as his senses were far keener than those of his younger companion. As the high-shouldered horses forged a path along the winding trail road, the massive Apache did not take his eyes off the dusty road.

Zococa knew that if there were danger of any kind in this hilly terrain, his partner would detect it long before he did and that suited the bandit.

Suddenly as the gelded grey cleared a giant shadow, Tahoka hauled back on his reins and stopped his mount. Before Zococa had drawn level to the grey horse, the giant Apache had dismounted.

The bandit steadied his pinto and stared down at his crouching pal. Zococa looped a leg over the stallion's mane and slid to the ground. Within three paces he was standing beside the thoughtful Apache.

'What is wrong, little one?' he asked as he vainly stared at the sand.

Tahoka turned his head abruptly. His emotionless features looked up at the colourful bandit as he swiftly talked with his fingers.

Zococa read the signals and felt a cold shiver trace his backbone. His eyes darted all around them and searched the pitch-black shadows.

'Are you sure, Tahoka?' he asked his kneeling companion.

The Apache grunted and rose to his full height. His hooded eyes also searched the moonlit boulders as well as the shadowy gaps between them. Tahoka talked again with his fingers as he reached back and grabbed the long leathers of his gelding. He pulled the horse toward him.

'You say that there are Apaches in this area?' Zococa questioned as he watched the muscular Indian mount the gelded grey.

Tahoka gave a violent nod of his head.

'But you are the only Apache within miles,' Zococa argued as he stepped into his stirrup and pulled himself back on to his saddle. 'This time I think you are wrong, *amigo*.'

The massive warrior swung his grey around and stared into the shadowy rocks. The mute Apache tapped his moccasins against the flanks of his mount and steered the tall animal toward some broken brush between two of the largest boulders.

Tahoka leaned forward and took hold of some of the dry branches and glared silently at them. Zococa eased his pinto stallion toward the wide shoulders of his friend and looked at the broken kindling in the massive hands.

As the Indian turned his head and stared at the unusually quiet bandit he pointed at the snapped length of brush. It was obvious to Zococa what his trusty comrade was indicating.

All moisture had been drained from the branch from where it had been broken. Tahoka threw the dead wood at the ground and then pointed between

86

the boulders. Zococa bit his lip and started to nod as he felt a bead of sweat rolling down his face.

'You are right, my little elephant,' he admitted. 'There are other Apaches in this area.'

It was obvious what Tahoka was gesturing about so feverishly as he grunted atop his powerful gelding. He wanted to hunt down the unseen Indians.

Zococa shook his head and turned his stallion to face the trail again. He waved his hand above his wide sombrero and started to continue their interrupted journey. The stallion had barely taken a forward step when Tahoka rode in front of him and frantically spoke with his large hands.

The handsome bandit read the unspoken words and then shook his head. He understood that the mute Apache wanted nothing more than to find the Indians who had mutilated him years before and left him to die staked out on a termite mound.

'We have more pressing work to do this night, Tahoka,' he calmly reminded his friend. 'We have to locate the pretty Isabella Sanchez and escort her back to Don Pedro. We have no time to waste by chasing shadows.'

Tahoka stared through the moonlight at his partner and snorted like a cornered bull. Vengeance was a bitter pill and like so many other medicines, it was addictive. Zococa knew that it had led the maimed Apache by the nose ever since he had saved Tahoka's life.

'We have no time,' Zococa repeated.

Tahoka reluctantly nodded. He dragged the head

of his grey around and aimed the feisty beast at the trail. The Apache knew that his younger companion was right.

The pair gathered up their reins and were about to slap their mounts into action when the surrounding rocks echoed with a deafening crescendo. Suddenly the horsemen watched as red hot tapers of lethal lead cut through the eerie darkness from all directions.

Rifle bullets rained down on them. Chunks of rock ricocheted off the boulders like a swarm of crazed hornets to both sides of the narrow pass.

The sound grew as more and more bullets flashed through the darkness and buried themselves into the sandy ground whilst others collided with the rocks to either side of the startled horsemen. No brass band could have created such a din and both the bandits had to strain every muscle they possessed just to keep their trusty mounts from bolting in terror.

They looked up at the moonlit top of the smooth boulders and saw the plumes of gunsmoke erupting from numerous rifles and then the colourful bandit spotted the distinctive sashes tied across the fore-heads of the shooters. Sashes designed to keep black manes of hair in place.

It was indeed Apaches, just like Tahoka had insisted.

Zococa and Tahoka leapt from their horses and rolled across the sand in a desperate bid to escape the deluge of death that was chasing them. They crawled to the boulders and drew their six-guns as they found a shadow to take refuge. Zococa fired up at the gunsmoke and watched as a warrior arched in agony and then toppled from his high vantage point.

The Indian fell like a rag doll. Both bandits watched as the limp figure hit the ground opposite them. A cloud of dust rose from around the body as his fellow Apaches continued to blast their rifles at their cornered prey.

'You were right, little one,' Zococa said as his eyes narrowed at the men far above them. 'There are Apaches around here.'

Tahoka raced from his partner to the gelded grey, dragged his repeating rifle from its saddle scabbard and then returned to the side of Zococa. The Indian cranked the Winchester's mechanism and grunted to himself before raising the weapon to his shoulder.

Zococa watched in stunned awe as the gigantic Tahoka expertly fired his rifle repeatedly at their attackers. Within a couple of minutes, Tahoka had emptied the Winchester's magazine and had started to reload.

'It might be better if you aimed, little elephant,' Zococa grinned before noticing that the Indians opposite had stopped firing. He got up on to his knees, pushed his sombrero back and squinted. 'Where did they go?'

Tahoka looked at his partner and then made a sign with his clenched fist before resuming his task of sliding fresh bullets into the smoking magazine.

Zococa raised an eyebrow. 'Are you telling me that you hit every one of those Indians?'

Tahoka grunted and then pushed the rifle's hand

guard down before abruptly returning it to the body of the Winchester. He edged away from the rock face and then, before Zococa could speak again, vanished into the shadows.

The bandit knew that, unlike himself, Tahoka was not prone to exaggeration. If he said that he had killed the Indians that he had been shooting at, then that was exactly what he had done.

After the brief lull in firing, the shooting started up again. Shots rained down from high above Zococa. The ground kicked up as countless bullets tore through the eerie light and peppered the ground a few feet away from Zococa. The bandit dragged the hammer of his pistol back until it locked and moved further along the rock wall.

Sweat trailed down his face as the bandit made a tentative break for the horses. Zococa had only taken two steps away from the protection of the rugged rocks when shots rang out and stopped him in his tracks. The high-shouldered pinto stallion, feeling the heat of the bullets behind its tail, raced away from its master. More deadly tapers tore down from above Zococa and ripped his sombrero from his head. As the wide-brimmed hat was sent spinning, the bandit threw himself sideways and fired his pistol in reply.

Smoke from the Apaches' rifles hung like a cloud of phantoms in the dry night air far above him. As Zococa squeezed his trigger again he caught a glimpse of something he recognized moving stealthily toward the three remaining Indians.

Before his thumb could pull back on his gun

hammer, Zococa heard a sickening noise drift down. The shooting had stopped because the Apaches had something far more pressing to deal with. Zococa quickly got to his feet, plucked his sombrero off the sand and then narrowed his eyes.

Although he could not see much from where he was standing, he could hear everything that was going on. The moans and screams chilled him to the bone.

He knew exactly what must be happening.

Then his suspicions were confirmed.

One by one the lifeless bodies of the Apaches were thrown off the high rocks. A line of crimson droplets hung in the night air and trailed the corpses through the moonlight. Zococa stepped aside as the dead Apaches crashed into the unforgiving ground beside him.

It was clear to Zococa that his silent friend had used all of his lethal weaponry in the destruction of the crumpled bodies beside him. He had seldom seen such savagery, but knew why Tahoka hated his fellow Apaches.

They had turned a noble warrior into something more akin to being a mutilated monster. He blamed each and every one of them as though they were personally responsible.

Zococa holstered his pistol and rubbed the grim expression from his handsome features. The Indians had tangled with his unforgiving *amigo*. They had paid the ultimate price and now had eternity to realize their error.

The two horses were still skittish as they stood

beside the famed bandit and pawed at the sand. Zococa gripped the long leathers tightly as his gigantic friend suddenly emerged from between two of the boulders and silently plodded toward his observer.

Tahoka remained emotionless as he thrust his rifle back into its rawhide saddle scabbard and then grabbed the mane of his awaiting mount. He mounted the horse and turned the animal to face the eastern trail.

Zococa often mocked his enormous sidekick, but knew when it was best not to say a word. This was such a time, he thought as he stepped into his stirrup and mounted the high-shouldered stallion. He gathered his reins and turned the pinto and patted the Apache on his back.

'Let us ride for Porta Quelbo, Tahoka,' he said. 'We have much time to make up.'

Both horsemen whipped their horses' flanks and spurred them into action. A cloud of trail dust rose into the night sky as their mounts thundered away from the sickening carnage.

TEN

Even before leaving the relative safety of Spain, detailed arrangements had been made for the smugglers' ship *Las Palmas* to bring its precious freight into the sheltered natural harbour known only to those who were used to bringing every known illicit cargo into its unsupervised coastal port.

Lush green mountainsides gave no clue as to what went on in the natural lagoon. Passing ships saw nothing but yet another tranquil inlet and that was exactly how seafarers and their landlocked counterparts liked it. Porta Quelbo would become totally valueless if its location and function were discovered by the authorities.

The gulf harbour had enough deep water for two wooden vessels to safely tie up against its floating pontoons. Normally only smugglers used the isolated port to either collect or drop their illicit freight but this day the grand wooden galleon carried an extra cargo.

A far more lucrative cargo.

One which Don Pedro Sanchez had paid a small fortune to be safely delivered to him. The captain and crew of the *Las Palmas* were some of the most brutal seafarers to sail the seven seas yet there were none more trustworthy. Don Pedro had selected them personally to escort his most precious possession from the old world to the new.

The ship had sailed to the very mouth of the natural harbour before the last rays of the sun fell from view. A crescent moon gave the sparkling waters the only illumination its skilled crew and captain needed.

Most ships the size of the vintage *Las Palmas* needed the lights of the towns to guide them into port safely but there were no such lights in the vicinity of Porta Quelbo. No lighthouses or other signs of humanity marked this secluded port and that suited everyone just fine.

To the outside world and to the Mexican government, Porta Quelbo simply did not exist. The ship sailed into the uncharted waters and slowly cruised toward the makeshift pontoon and the awaiting locals.

As the massive wooden vessel neared the floating pontoons, scores of torches suddenly erupted into life as the shore-side stevedores put matches to them.

Light marked the quayside and spilled out onto the quiet waters. It was just enough for the large vessel to aim at. What might have seemed like a terribly difficult and dangerous manoeuvre to most deep-sea vessels was nothing to this regular visitor.

Scores of ropes were thrown from the *Las Palmas* down to the awaiting hands of the men on the pontoon. One by one they secured the ropes and then started to speedily pull the ship toward the pontoon.

Every single man knew their duties and what was expected of them and was eager to start work. The *Las Palmas* was famed for its speedy turnaround and normally it would be back at sea less than hour after arriving, but its seasoned master realized there might be a delay due to his unusual cargo. The vintage vessel did not usually carry passengers.

Captain Ferdinand Costa had spent more than forty years on the high seas and been the master of the huge *Las Palmas* for the previous decade. There was nothing this veteran seafarer had not seen or done during his days on the seven seas and he had become a legend in his own lifetime. Costa was known throughout the Mexican gulf and beyond for his uncanny skill at outwitting the authorities and never failing to deliver his cargo.

Yet as he stared into the flickering torchlight below the quarterdeck of the *Las Palmas*, Costa wondered if accepting the enormous fee Don Pedro had paid him might prove costly.

Time was of the essence in his dubious profession and he knew that even a few moments delay in casting off might prove deadly. Mexican government vessels navigated the eastern coast looking for smugglers and would fire their cannons at any ship they suspected of evading duty.

Being trapped in a cove like Porta Quelbo was not desirable.

The wily sea captain knew that only back at sea was there any safety for him and his crew. He brooded on what he should do if Isabella Sanchez's escort failed to arrive at the quayside when their cargo had been unloaded. He did not want to keep her on the ship and take her back to Spain, but wondered how safe she might be if he left her ashore when they cast off again.

The multitude of ropes tightened as the *Las Palmas* was hauled to the pontoons and tied off. Within seconds, gangplanks were lowered and muscular men readied themselves.

Captain Costa stood on the quarterdeck and watched his crew and the smugglers steady the ship and prepare for the unloading of its illicit goods. It was a well-oiled machine which practice had honed to perfection.

As if from nowhere, a dozen or more wagons suddenly came into view about fifty yards away from the starboard side of the *Las Palmas*. Costa rested his hands on the wooden bulkhead and squinted hard at the unlit township nestled in the mass of trees.

Porta Quelbo never advertised its existence to the outside world when they were expecting a ship to call. The captain said nothing as his expert crewmen started to unload its cargo of rum and other delicacies at incredible speed. The two gangplanks rocked as men moved in quick succession up and down their planking. The seafarer lit a pipe and inhaled its strong smoke as he thought about the even more valuable freight he had below deck.

He knew that the two females were a lot tougher than most he had escorted across the vast oceans. The older one was well past her best and a mere chaperone for the far younger beauty he had enjoyed the pleasure of dining with for the duration of the long trip.

For the first time in his entire life, he was going to regret bidding farewell to the younger of the pair. Isabella Sanchez was the most handsome female he had ever set eyes upon and as feisty as they came.

She was no delicate wallflower.

Isabella had guts and courage in abundance. She was the sort of female that would put up her fists and fight and the captain admired that.

Both the women were obeying his strict orders and remained out of sight as his crew speedily emptied the ship's holds of its cargo. Captain Costa pulled the pipe stem from his craggy lips and ran his fingers over his white shaggy beard. For years he had prided himself on his well-trimmed beard and waxed moustache, but that had been a long time ago.

Now he was content just to be who he was. An old sea captain closer to death than he was to life.

All he wanted now was to earn as much money as he could before he retired from his precarious profession. His one desire was to find himself a secluded desert island to await the Grim Reaper in style.

He considered the females below decks and fretted.

Don Pedro's written instructions had been

detailed. Costa knew that he was sending an agent to Porta Quelbo to meet his daughter and her servant. The agent would then escort the beautiful Isabella and her maid back to El Sanchez.

The seasoned seafarer was well aware of the danger that the females and the escort faced. There were many ways to die between the coastal port and the famed El Sanchez, and Don Pedro's enemies would attempt to enlist every one of them.

Captain Costa marched down the steps from the quarterdeck to the open holds. He glanced into the depths of his ship and nodded in satisfaction to himself. Most of his cargo had already been taken ashore. He checked his pocket watch and nodded in mute satisfaction.

'You're doing well, lads,' he encouraged and clapped his hands together. 'You'll all have plenty of rum when we set sail again.'

As the bearded man watched his crew feverishly going about their duties, he glanced at the quayside again and then snapped the lid of his gold hunter shut.

'That agent better arrive soon,' he muttered under his breath as he moved to the rail. 'I'd hate to have to leave them women on the quayside when we set sail.'

As the master of the *Las Palmas* tapped his hands together behind his back, he doubted if he could just abandon the females in such a place.

ELEVEN

The pair of horsemen might not have even suspected that they were actually close to the vast gulf of starlit water had it not been for the wide road which they were travelling along. As Zococa eased back on his reins and slowed the pinto stallion, he heard the familiar sound of wagon chains rattling somewhere ahead of them. Tahoka had heard the sound of the wagons long before his flamboyant companion and had drawn his six-shooter as the noise grew louder.

The bandits steered their mounts off the road and took refuge in the dense undergrowth. Zococa rested a hand on a nearby tree trunk as the nervous Apache warrior glared at the dark shadowy road.

'Calm down, little one,' Zococa said calmly as his narrowed eyes watched the blackness in anticipation. 'We have done enough killing for one night.'

As the warrior heeded the words, a wagon cleared the dense tree lined road and rolled passed them. Both horsemen studied the flatbed behind the two men on the driver's board. A massive canvas sheet covered whatever was secreted beneath it.

Zococa raised his eyebrows as three more equally laden wagon rolled passed the bandits. If he had not already agreed to undertake escorting Isabella Sanchez back to her father, he might have been tempted to steal one of the rattling wagons.

'I wonder what they have hidden under those oil sheets, Tahoka,' Zococa grinned at his pal. 'It might be valuable.'

The Apache holstered his six-gun and rode his grey out from the trees. He glanced over his shoulder at his fellow bandit as Zococa trailed him.

The riders rode into the avenue of trees and rode through the darkness down a steep hillside. As the horsemen cleared the surrounding trees and emerged back in the moonlight, they suddenly saw the large ship. The light of countless stars twinkled like dancing jewels upon the harbour water as both riders cantered down to the floating pontoons.

'I think we have found it, *amigo*,' Zococa announced in a surprised tone as their mounts walked on to the gently swaying pontoon and started making their way past a dozen or more seafarers toward the closest gangplank.

Large barrels of rum and other tropical spirits were still being rolled down from the ship's deck to the awaiting stevedores before being transferred over the planks on to the last of the awaiting wagons.

Zococa removed his silver case, flicked open its lid and plucked a cigar from within its body. He placed the long black stick of tobacco between his lips and then struck a match. As he returned the case to his pocket, the bandit's eyes flashed at the watching men amid the cargo. Some were locals but most were obviously hardened seafarers by the cut of their distinctive clothing.

'We seem to be attracting much attention, little one,' Zococa commented as he struck a match across his ornate saddle horn. 'I am most flattered.'

Suddenly, without warning, the burly men to either side of the tall-shouldered horses sprang into action and rushed both bandits in a fevered fury. They grappled and then dragged the startled horsemen off their saddles. Zococa and Tahoka hit the wooden boards hard and felt the water splash up between the pontoon's timbers.

The majority of them concentrated on the massive Tahoka and fought like demons to subdue the Apache. The remainder held the colourful bandit by his limbs and rested upon Zococa's heaving chest until he stopped wriggling. Tahoka stared at the knives and bailing hooks poised above him and then stopped resisting as well.

'Do not gut them, *amigos*,' Captain Costa yelled out. His booming voice carried well in the crisp night air as he followed his words down to the makeshift jetty. 'I am expecting someone and this pair might be them.'

Costa glared down at the heavily restrained bandits and smiled broadly at them. He moved away from the gigantic Apache to where Zococa lay beneath the muscular men.

'Release him,' Costa ordered.

The master of the *Las Palmas* watched in amusement as Zococa removed the broken cigar from his lips and looked around at the well-drilled men. He carefully got back to his feet and adjusted his clothing before staring at Costa.

'Don Pedro did not tell me that you travel with an army of very angry *amigos*, Captain.' Zococa moved to where the mighty Apache warrior lay beneath the muscular men and then cast his unsmiling face at the ship's master. 'Tell your cut-throats to let my little elephant go as well.'

Captain Costa walked the way all seafarers did and swayed unsteadily with each step. The bearded master of the *Las Palmas* pulled the pipe from his lips and focused hard on the famed bandit. He jabbed the air and pointed the pipe stem at the huge Indian.

'I was not told to expect you travelling with a giant Indian and this disturbs me,' Costa hissed as his eyes inspected the flamboyant character before him. 'You might not even be who I am expecting. You might be one of Don Pedro's mortal enemies.'

Zococa raised his eyebrows. He imagined that everyone knew of the great Zococa and would never doubt his word.

'I am not one of Don Pedro's villainous foes, Captain,' he said firmly. 'My name is Luis Santiago Rodrigo Vallencio, the famed bandit known as Zococa. I have diced with death on both sides of the border and am wanted dead or alive in both countries.'

Costa grinned at the obvious outrage.

'Who is he?' he asked pointing at the massive Apache. 'Don Pedro did not inform me that you were travelling with an Indian.'

Zococa inhaled deeply and appeared to actually grow before the veteran seafarer. 'That is Tahoka, my comrade and fellow bandit. He is never far from my side and has saved my life as many times as I have saved his.'

Captain Costa rubbed his whiskers before returning the pipe to his mouth and sucking the last of its flavoursome smoke from its hot bowl. He snapped his fingers at the men who straddled the Indian warrior and watched as they quickly released their frantic grip on Tahoka.

The snorting brave clambered back to his feet and straightened up to his full, impressive height. It was obvious to the bandits that Costa had never seen anyone as large as the angry Tahoka.

Captain Costa's eyes widened as he took a backward step.

'Good grief, he's a giant,' the ship's master stammered. 'I see why you travel with him, Zococa. He is the size of two or more men.'

Zococa's eyes darted between the numerous faces surrounding them as Tahoka plucked the reins of their horses off the damp boards and then stood behind his cohort. It was as if each and every one of the gathering suddenly became aware of how enormous the Indian they had dragged off his grey mount was.

103

Zococa glanced at the ship and then back at Costa.

'We are here to escort the daughter of Don Pedro back to El Sanchez,' he reminded the captain. 'Could you please inform the beautiful Isabella that the greatest bandit in all of Mexico awaits her company, *señor*?'

'You shall require a carriage for the ladies, Zococa,' Costa said bluntly as he turned back toward the gangplank. 'They are not dressed to ride on the backs of your horses.'

Zococa tilted his head. 'Excuse me, *señor.*'

'What?' Captain Costa asked with a glance over his shoulder as he placed a shoe on the bottom of the wooden companionway.

'Ladies?' There was a hint of surprise in the bandit's voice as he repeated the simple word. 'What do you mean by ladies? We were just expecting the very pretty Isabella. Who is this other female that we know nothing about?'

Captain Costa gave the confused bandit the broadest grin that Zococa had ever seen in his entire life. He did not answer the question but gave two of his motley crew a signal, which they obviously understood. Both men ran along the jetty toward the well-hidden settlement.

Zococa and Tahoka were equally dumbfounded.

'Stay here with the horses, little one,' Zococa said before ascending the gangplank in long strides. Before Captain Costa had reach the ship's quarterdeck, the bandit caught up with the seafarer.

Costa stopped at the top of the wide plank and

looked at the youthful bandit in surprise. He swung around and plucked his pipe from his mouth before asking, 'What do you want, Zococa?'

Zococa removed his sombrero and edged slightly forward. He then cleared his throat and glanced at the rugged-looking crewmen as they continued with their duties.

'I want you to explain a couple of things to me, *señor*,' Zococa started nervously. 'Don Pedro did not mention two females when he sent Tahoka and myself on this dangerous mission. Who is the other lady?'

Costa peered like an eagle through his bushy eyebrows at the bandit. Zococa might have been a famed bandit but he was completely out of his depth, the captain silently reasoned.

'You will discover who the other lady is, Zococa,' he simply stated and then rubbed his beard with his left hand. 'I'm sure she will enlighten you.'

Zococa did not understand the seafarer's words but it sounded interesting. He edged a little closer to Costa as the master of the *Las Palmas* rested his hands on the side of the ship and looked down at the activity below.

'This other lady sounds interesting, Captain,' he said. 'I am not unfamiliar with the fairer sex.'

Costa lashed out with his free arm and caught the bandit in his belly. Zococa coughed as the captain then indicated for him to look below them. Zococa stared down at the vehicle which had been driven to the foot of the gangplank.

It was an enclosed black carriage drawn by a sturdy horse and was being carefully driven by one of Costa's crewmen. Zococa had not even considered how he and Tahoka were going to safely transport the beautiful Isabella back to El Sanchez until this very moment.

'Don Pedro provided me with ample funds to pay for his daughter's passage and for a suitable vehicle for her to travel in, Zococa.' Costa spat and watched as a lump of dark goo floated through the torchlight before landing between the horses below. 'All you have to do is ensure that she survives.'

The words were simple enough but sounded daunting to the bandit as he toyed with the wide brim of his hat. He suddenly wondered what his fate might be should Don Pedro's enemies succeed in their deadly plans to prevent Isabella from reaching her destination.

'We have already encountered some of Don Pedro's enemies on our trip here, Captain,' Zococa revealed. 'What would happen to my little elephant and myself should the lovely Isabella fall foul of his enemy's wrath?'

Costa turned to face the bandit and tutted.

'If she dies, then you will also die, Zococa,' he stated firmly. 'You must protect her with every last drop of your blood or the ruler of El Sanchez will have you hung, drawn and quartered.'

Zococa was about to speak when a door across the deck swung open and a short, stout female clad entirely in black emerged on to the quarterdeck. She glanced across the distance between herself and the captain and started toward him.

Without taking his eyes off the advancing female, Zococa plucked the tiny portrait from his pocket and stared at it beautiful image.

'She looks a lot slimmer in this picture, Captain,' Zococa gasped in disbelief as his eyes darted between the image on the brooch and the reality that was heading toward them. 'She also looks a lot older in real life.'

Captain Costa was amused by the stunned expression etched into his young companion's face. He patted Zococa on the back and sighed heavily.

'Do not be disheartened, *amigo*,' he said. 'Nothing is ever as it seems.'

TWELVE

The rotund middle-aged female passed both Zococa and the grinning ship's master without uttering a word. The bandit watched as she stepped on the gangplank and waddled down to where the carriage was standing. She waved a heavily scented kerchief at the horses and the massive Apache warrior before returning it to her nose and entering the vehicle.

The mute Tahoka held the bridles of the horses and glanced up at his equally bemused friend. Even the torchlight could not conceal the disappointment in Zococa's face.

Zococa waved the miniature portrait under Costa's nose angrily and complained loudly.

'This is what Don Pedro and myself thought the lovely Isabella looks like,' he scowled before dropping the handsome brooch back into his pocket. 'That female looks older than her father. I do not understand. I am most disappointed.'

Captain Costa glanced at the deflated bandit.

'I imagine that you and that gigantic Indian might

108

not have risked your necks for that little fat lady,' he said as his keen ears heard a further set of footsteps inside the body of the vessel. 'Am I right, Zococa?'

'*Sí, señor*,' Zococa confessed and then sighed heavily. 'I hoped that she might at least look something like the painted image.'

Costa raised his arm and pointed to the slender creature who had just stepped out on to the quarter-deck and was sauntering toward them.

'If you look over there I think you will agree with me that the Lady Isabella looks exactly like her portrait,' the bearded man said in an amused tone.

Zococa glanced up and suddenly saw the most beautiful female his eyes had ever set sight upon. The bandit watched in stunned awe as she appeared to float toward the captain. There was a strange twinkle in her eyes that seemed to relish the torchlight that cast its amber illumination across the deck.

'Lady Isabella,' Costa gave a slight bow and then gestured to the gangplank. 'Your carriage awaits.'

Isabella gave a slight smile and then looked at the handsome bandit who had fallen silent since first seeing her. She reached out and closed his mouth with a gloved finger.

'Are you the escort?' she asked.

Zococa wanted to speak, but only managed to nod.

'This is the great Zococa, my dear lady,' Captain Costa informed her. 'Your father considers him to be the most trustworthy bandit in all of Mexico.'

'Are you dangerous, Zococa?' her gentle voice teased the tall bandit. 'You look as if you might be very dangerous.'

Zococa shrugged.

'I think so, pretty lady,' he managed to say before adding. 'I am also most attractive to many beautiful *señoritas.*'

She concealed her amusement at his unease and boastful statement with a small square of black lace that she dabbed her lips with.

'I feel safer now that I have met with you, Zococa,' she purred like a cat and then placed her hand on his arm. 'Now you may take me to the vehicle.'

Zococa dutifully led Isabella Sanchez down the gangplank toward the carriage and then ushered her into the confines of the black vehicle. No sooner had they stepped off the wooden companionway than the crew hastily released the ropes and ascended back on to the ship.

The mighty ship dropped its sails and, as the evening breeze filled its canvas, slowly sailed away from the quayside. The flamboyant bandit watched in awe as within a few minutes, the wooden vessel made its way back to the open sea.

With a respectful bow, Zococa closed the carriage door and touched his hat brim to the attractive young lady sat beside her grim-faced chaperone before signally to the driver perched at the rear of the vehicle.

The driver cracked his reins above the stationary horse between its traces and slowly turned the carriage as Zococa and Tahoka mounted their horses.

'I shall ride ahead of the vehicle,' he told the mighty Apache as he gathered up the slack of his long leathers. 'You follow and keep your eyes peeled for trouble, little one.'

Tahoka nodded firmly.

With its escorts at either end of its compact length, the black carriage started to move slowly along the floating pontoon toward the secreted settlement.

As the silent *Las Palmas* expertly navigated out into the gulf, each of the torches that had guided it into the natural harbour was extinguished, returning Porta Quelbo to obscurity.

Zococa tapped his spurs into the flanks of his pinto mount and encouraged his muscular stallion up the tree-lined slope with the black carriage in close pursuit. With every stride of his powerful horse, the normally carefree bandit felt an unease washing over him.

It had not been until he had met the breath-taking female that Zococa had suddenly realized the enormity of his and Tahoka's mission.

If this went wrong, she would surely die.

Zococa felt a cold shiver trace his backbone.

This was a mission he simply had to get right, he told himself. There was no room for error and he vowed that her enemies would have to kill him before they ever reached her.

They rolled on.

THIRTEEN

The ambitious Don Ricardo led his small army of deadly *vaqueros* on a different course to the one taken by the intrepid Zococa and his mute companion. Whilst the bandits had opted for a route which had a trail that was regarded as the far more direct to the distant gulf coast, Don Ricardo and his men had chosen the far safer route to and from El Sanchez.

The thirty or so horsemen knew that their journey would be longer than the one taken by Zococa, but it was far safer. As far as Don Ricardo was concerned only a fool or a madman would have taken the trail through swamplands and territory known to be inhabited by rampaging Apaches.

Yet as the overly ambitious nobleman led his riders down through a canyon pass where, his trusty henchman José Manilla had informed him, he had sent six of his best *vaqueros* in order to bushwhack the mysterious bandit, Don Ricardo's eyes widened.

Even the darkness could not disguise the horror that was etched into Don Ricardo's face. He dragged his reins back and slowed his outriders as he stared at the bodies strewn across the canyon floor.

'What is wrong, Don Ricardo?' Manilla called out from his trusty mount.

Without uttering a word, Don Ricardo raised his arm and pointed through the eerie moonlight toward the black lumps that littered the ground between the blackest of shadows.

Manilla swung his horse around and squinted hard.

Then he too saw the sickening sight. Large buzzards hopped like jackrabbits between the bodies as they dined on their unexpected feast.

'I see dead men, *señor*,' Manilla gasped in surprise. 'Many dead men.'

Don Ricardo thrust his spurs into the flanks of his mount and thundered forward with his men flanking his every stride. As the horses neared the bodies, the large birds flapped their massive wings and flew away from their meal. Lumps of flesh fell from their savage beaks.

The nobleman drew back on his reins and stopped his mighty stallion just above the closest of the stricken bodies. He stared down in disbelief at the horrific sight and then glared at Manilla.

'Are these the bandits or are they the remains of our men, José?' Don Ricardo snarled as he caught the sickening stench of the entrails that had been torn from crumpled bodies. 'Tell me quickly before I am violently sick.'

Manilla and a handful of their men dismounted

and moved swiftly to the bodies. It only took a few moments for them to identify the *vaqueros*.

'They are the men I sent to ambush Don Pedro's escorts, *señor*,' Manilla said in a trembling voice.

Don Ricardo watched as Manilla turned his head and looked across the moonlit sand desperately. The hired gunman rubbed his neck nervously.

'What are you looking for, José?' Don Ricardo asked.

Manilla glanced from under his sombrero at the face of his leader and shrugged as he carefully stepped over the body parts strewn all around them.

'There were more of them, Don Ricardo,' he replied.

Don Ricardo sighed. 'They must be dead as well, José. I do not think that these bandits would have left any of our *vaqueros* alive.'

With sweat rolling down his face, Manilla mounted and gathered up his long leathers before watching the large black buzzards fly up to the cliff overhangs.

Suddenly the sound of fighting birds drew the attention of every one of the horsemen. Then without warning another body fell from the top of the canyon wall and came crashing to the ground beside one of the others.

A cloud of dust rose off the ground as the lifeless *vaquero* stared up at his still-living comrades.

The *vaqueros* steadied their skittish mounts as they listened to the haunting noises far above them. Manilla rubbed the sweat off his face with the back of his jacket sleeve and looked at Don Ricardo.

'You are right, Don Ricardo,' Manilla croaked as his gripped his reins firmly. 'The bandits killed them all.'

'They shall pay for what they have done, José.' Don Ricardo had the reality of the situation thrust into his single-minded brain yet he still thought that what he was intending to do was worth it. Men cut from the same cloth as the evil nobleman never questioned their own motives. It was others who were always wrong.

Manilla studied the ground and could see two sets of hoof marks in the sand leading from where the group of riders were gathered.

'They headed that way, *señor,*' he told Don Ricardo with a gesture. 'There are only two of them.'

'Two very dangerous bandits who know how to use their pistols by the evidence they have littered the sand with, José,' Don Ricardo corrected as he allowed his white stallion to walk in the same direction that the tracks were leading. 'We shall follow them and. . . .'

Manilla and several of the other horsemen interrupted their paymaster before he could finish his statement. They cleared their throats loudly and drew Don Ricardo's attention.

'I know the bandits went in that direction, *señor,*' the *vaquero* stated as he encouraged his own horse closer to the white stallion. 'The trouble is that they are heading straight into land which is an Apache stronghold. We dare not follow.'

'No stinking Indians can stop Don Ricardo from

115

following those two, José,' the irate Sanchez roared angrily. 'I am not afraid.'

Manilla rested the palms of his hands on his saddle horn and sighed heavily before whispering to his leader in a tone which could not be heard by the other horsemen behind them.

'There are two more trails to the coast, Don Ricardo,' he said as his eyes darted at the moonlit features. 'To take this trail is suicide. I thought you wished to kill the bastard daughter of your brother? Is this not so?'

'You know it is, José,' Don Ricardo hissed.

'It will be us that die if we follow these hoof tracks, *señor*,' Manilla added. 'Not the girl. I know another trail which will avoid the Apaches and still get us to the coast.'

Don Ricardo reluctantly accepted the logic of his underling's words and snorted as he glanced back at the riders behind them. His eyes flashed at Manilla.

'What do you suggest, José?' he asked.

Manilla swung his mount around and faced their small army of heavily-armed horsemen. He stood in his stirrups and started waving his arms at the watchful riders.

Within a mere minute he had sent two groups of the heavily-armed horsemen to various trails with orders to kill anyone they encountered. As he lowered himself back on to his saddle, he had eight of his most notorious gunmen still watching and waiting for their instructions. Even the darkness which enveloped them like cloaks could not conceal the troubled expressions on their faces. They had seen what Zococa and his partner could do with their six-guns and were wary of encountering the same fate.

Manilla grinned at the horsemen.

'You shall come with Don Ricardo and myself, *amigos*,' he shouted as he turned his horse and nodded to the watchful rider of the large white stallion. 'I have *vaqueros* heading to all of the other trails the bandits might use to escort the young female to El Sanchez, *señor*. If Don Pedro's daughter travels along any of those trails, they will all die.'

'You have all the trail roads covered,' Don Ricardo frowned at his trusty henchman as he gripped his reins tightly. 'All except this trail that you claim heads through Apache land, José.'

'If the bandits have survived I doubt that they would repeat their mistake and return along this particular trail,' Manilla said bluntly. 'I know a far safer route for us to use to reach the coast. With any luck we shall bump into your niece and her escorts on the road. If the bandits were slain by the Apaches, then we will meet up with your brother's daughter in or around Porta Quelbo. She will be alone and waiting for your brother's agents. Either way, she is doomed.'

A cruel smile crossed Don Ricardo's face. His thoughts drifted to the innocent Isabella and the fate he had intended for her. His grin grew wider as he signalled to the horsemen behind them.

'Come on, *amigos*,' he rallied his troops with a sweeping gesture of his arm. 'We ride to ensure that El Sanchez has only one true contender to its throne and that is me.'

The *vaqueros* cheered their leader and cracked their long leathers across the tails of their mounts and followed both Don Ricardo and Manilla down through an avenue of tall trees and windy trails.

FOURTEEN

The previous few years had seen the flamboyant Zococa expand his reputation to almost breath-taking heights. He had wanted nothing more than to be regarded as the most famous bandit ever to draw breath, but now as he led the small caravan back along the trail he and Tahoka had taken to reach the secluded Porta Quelbo, he started to doubt whether he and his trusty Apache friend were capable of fending off a mass attack by more than a handful of *vaqueros* or Indians.

He was unusually nervous.

Zococa's eyes darted around the trail as the mighty pinto stallion cantered through the eerie moonlight as it obeyed its master's spurs. Every few strides of the muscular mount, Zococa glanced back at the black carriage which was following him closely and the emotionless face of Tahoka bringing up the rear a few yards behind the vehicle's wheels.

The carriage driver sat high above the enclosed coach at the back of the well-sprung vehicle and

watched the famed bandit carefully. The eerie moonlight danced across the small man's concerned face as
he watched Zococa and matched his speed. As always
the mute Apache warrior watched everything before
him with a stony silence. His hooded eyes never
appearing to blink or stray from those he was determined to protect.

So far they had not encountered any trouble, but
the closer they got to the fabled El Sanchez, the more
anxious the famed bandit was becoming. Zococa
knew that his reputation meant nothing in this
unusual scenario and he was well aware that the
reclusive Don Ricardo Sanchez was a man who would
do anything he could to prevent his brother's daughter from ever reaching or inheriting El Sanchez.

Zococa and his trusty friend had already encountered some of Don Ricardo's hired killers. Everything
pointed to the fact that there would be more.

Many more.

He had to protect the beautiful Lady Isabella from
an enemy who was unknown to him. He had learned
that Don Pedro's brother was intent on preventing
the innocent female from ever reaching the famed El
Sanchez.

Zococa was well aware that no amount of exaggeration on his part could stop a hoard of deadly
attackers. He would not be able to bluff this enemy as
he had done with so many others over the years. He
would somehow have to fight and protect the innocent young female in a way which was totally alien to
his normally flamboyant manner.

He was always confident when it was just himself and Tahoka riding into unknown territories. But this was a far more risky game than anything he had ever contemplated previously.

There was the beautiful Isabella to consider.

He had never set eyes upon anyone like her before and it confused the bandit. She was more than just a painted image now to the virile Zococa. Isabella was flesh and blood.

She was real.

This was totally different for the renowned bandit as he had someone else to consider and protect besides just Tahoka and his own hide. Zococa had the lovely Isabella and her plump chaperone to consider and that troubled him.

Zococa had vowed to Don Pedro that he would give his life to protect the ravishing female and now realized that he might have to do just that.

How many more *vaqueros* loyal to the ruthless Don Ricardo might be heading to ambush his priceless charge? The question gnawed at his innards as he continued to lead the black carriage further and further away from Porta Quelbo.

The southpaw eased back on his reins for a moment and allowed the coach to roll past him as he waited for the grim-faced Tahoka to draw level with him. Zococa rode beside the mighty Apache warrior as they ventured deeper into the dense overgrown landscape.

'Soon we will be returning to the land of your fellow Apaches, Tahoka,' the bandit said as they finally cleared the trees and started toward the gigantic boulders. 'I am afraid that if they attack the carriage, the females will be slaughtered.'

Tahoka narrowed his hooded eyes and glared ahead of them at the rocks they were speedily approaching. Suddenly the fearless warrior whipped his gelded grey with the loose ends of his reins and galloped away from his colourful comrade.

Zococa watched in stunned bewilderment as Tahoka thundered away from his pinto stallion, passed the black carriage and then disappeared into the evening shadows.

The bandit spurred his pinto and drew level with the fast-moving carriage. He looked up at the vehicle's driver and gave a nod of his head.

'How far is it to El Sanchez, Zococa?' the driver shouted down from his lofty perch. 'When will we get there? I am scared of this land.'

'You are not alone, *amigo*,' Zococa admitted as his eyes vainly searched for the gigantic Apache warrior. 'There are a thousand places for spineless ambushers to shoot from and we are moving right into the heart of it.'

The driver did not like the words he had just heard. He cracked his whip above the head of his horse and then looked down upon the bandit.

'At least you are honest,' he gulped.

The bandit evaluated the situation as his fertile mind wondered where his massive friend had gone. Zococa looked up to the driver and gave his best guess.

'We should be there in about another hour, *amigo*,' he answered dryly as he glimpsed the two females inside the small coach. Lady Isabella smiled at the horseman and then hid behind a black fan.

'Where did your friend go in such a hurry, Zococa?' the driver asked the famed bandit. 'I have never seen anyone ride so fast. Was he running away? Has he deserted us?'

'Tahoka never runs away, *amigo*,' Zococa corrected. 'He is a warrior and always faces his demons. He is the bravest soul I have ever known.'

The bandit decided to try and attempt to encourage the vulnerable coach driver as he firmly gripped his reins. He smiled broadly as thoughts of the unpredictable Apaches returned to his mind.

'The trail is tricky up ahead, *amigo*,' Zococa bluffed. 'You must be careful.'

The driver cracked his whip above the head of the solitary horse between the vehicle's traces and looked down at the smiling face of the bandit. This was the first time that he had seen the normally confident bandit so subdued.

Then without warning Zococa thrust his spurs into the flanks of his powerful mount and raced away from the carriage. Suddenly the night sky grew even darker as storm clouds began to gather across the heavens above the bandit. The scent of a gathering storm filled Zococa's flared nostrils as he searched for his large comrade amid the massive boulders.

The bandit looked down at the ground but could not make out any tell-tale signs of the gelded grey's

123

hoof tracks. The sand across which he and the silent Apache had travelled on their way to the coast was now churned up.

'Many riders have cut through this pass,' Zococa told himself as the hairs on the nape of his neck started to tingle a warning to him. His eyes flashed around the surrounding area, but it was growing darker with every beat of his thumping heart before adding. 'And all their hoofs are unshod.'

Zococa pulled back on his reins, stopped the mount and listened to the carriage catch up with his snorting pinto stallion. As the carriage passed the stationary bandit, Zococa looked up at the vast heavens. Star after star vanished from sight and then the moon was also blanketed by the dense black clouds.

In the distance he could see bright flashes of lightning.

There was a strange smell in the air. It had the aroma of burning and was familiar to the young horseman. He watched helplessly as everything around him grew blacker and blacker within seconds.

The mighty stallion beneath him started to buck, but the expert horseman held it in check.

'Easy, horse,' he told the stallion as it strained at the reins gripped in his hands. 'It is just the gods flexing their muscles.'

Before the words had left his lips the entire area was blanketed in a blackness that chilled him. Zococa loosened his grip on the long leathers and allowed the stallion to race after the carriage. Within seconds, the powerful pinto had caught up with the vehicle as it slowed to a virtual halt in the middle of the trail road.

Zococa dragged back on his reins.

A cloud of dust plumed up from his horse's hoofs as the stallion abruptly stopped beside the carriage. Zococa looked up at the driver, but could hardly see the small man.

It was darker than the bandit had ever experienced. Giant rocks and impressive trees only added to the depth of the darkness. Zococa swung his mount full circle as he still vainly searched for any sign of his silent friend.

'Why did you stop me driving on, Zococa?' the small man perched high on the driver's seat asked.

'I'm not sure, *amigo*,' Zococa admitted as he looked back at the rods of lethal power that were snaking down from the clouds behind them. 'I think it might be wise to wait for Tahoka to return before we continue our journey.'

'What if he doesn't return?' the stammering driver's voice asked. 'I've heard tales that there are Indians in these mountains.'

A distant flash of lightning briefly lit up Zococa's face as he frowned thoughtfully. Zococa shook his head and moved his powerful stallion closer to the carriage.

'If there are any Apaches around here,' he started, 'Tahoka will surely kill them, *amigo*.'

The coach driver toyed with his long reins, which covered the roof of the vehicle and stretched out to the horse between its wooden traces.

125

'But ain't he an Apache?'

Zococa nodded. 'He is, but he hates them.'

'Why?' the driver looked puzzled.

'Why? It was his fellow Apaches that cut his tongue from his mouth and he has vowed to destroy them all for that outrage, *amigo*,' the bandit replied as the blackness overwhelmed him again. 'Tahoka is not a man to argue with when it comes to Apaches.'

The small man perched on his high seat pulled the collar of his coat up as a stiff breeze swept between the huge boulders and rocked the carriage. The thought of Apaches chilled the driver to the bone.

'I do not like this place, Zococa,' he stammered in a tone which the bandit recognized. 'I have the feeling that death lurks around this place.'

The handsome bandit held the long leathers firmly in his right hand as his left stroked the ivory grip of his holstered pistol. He knew only too well that his gigantic friend was hunting down his fellow Apaches somewhere in the rocks that surrounded them. Tahoka would not return until he had dispatched his own brand of vengeance upon them.

'You are correct, *amigo*,' Zococa agreed with a gentle nod of his head. 'Death lurks in this place.'

Before the driver could reply, Zococa eased back on his long leathers and allowed the stallion to walk backwards until he was level with the carriage door. It was impossible for him to see anything within the coach as he leaned from his saddle and peered inside.

'Are you all right, pretty lady?' he whispered as

though some unseen enemy might be close enough to overhear. 'Do not let the darkness trouble you.'

'Who is this ruffian, Isabella?' the harsh voice of Isabella's chaperone cut through the silence. 'Why is he with us and why are we travelling with that filthy savage?'

Zococa frowned. He did not like anyone talking about the fearless Tahoka that way and was about to unleash a tirade of verbal abuse back at her when the seductive voice of the beautiful Isabella floated from the coach and washed over him.

'Do not talk to the great Zococa like that, Maria,' Isabella scolded her companion, to the amusement of the bandit. 'He is risking his life by travelling with us to El Sanchez.'

Maria del Rio was a spinster who had always looked down her nose at every man she had encountered over the years. As her hair had changed from that of a raven's wing to something as white as snow, she had grown even more critical. The rotund chaperone had been engaged to escort the ravishing female from their native Spain to Mexico and had hated every second of the trip.

She growled from the dark corner of the coach interior at her youthful charge in a way only those whose souls are as twisted as their faces can do.

'But why must he travel with a godless creature like that stinking Indian?' the chaperone asked with a hog-like snort. 'I could smell that filthy wretch from the deck of the ship.'

The beautiful female was angrier than she had ever

been as the older woman added even more venomous words to her outburst.

'I would not be surprised if we were both assaulted
and cut into tiny slivers, Isabella,' the chaperone said.
'Mark my words. We shall never reach El Sanchez.
They will kill us after they have satisfied their carnal
cravings. No men can be trusted.'

'You are quite safe, Maria,' Isabella retorted. 'Only
a fool would even try to ravish you and I do not think
my father hires fools.'

Without warning, the door of the small carriage
burst open and Zococa could hear the ruffling of
clothing as the furious Isabella descended to the
ground. Zococa found his box of matches and then
struck one and cupped its flickering flame.

The temporary light lit up the handsome features
of the female who was a hundred times more beautiful than the painted image that he kept close to his
heart. The match expired as Zococa threw his leg
over the head of the pinto and slid to the ground. He
reached out and caught hold of Isabella's hands.

'You are trembling, little lady,' Zococa noted.

'I am angry, Zococa,' she admitted. 'That creature
has driven me out of my mind since she was first
retained.'

The bandit shrugged. 'I understand.'

'What are you doing, Isabella?' the rotund female
inside the carriage snorted in a disapproving tone.
'Get back inside this coach at once.'

Zococa turned his back to Maria del Rio. His wide-
brimmed sombrero prevented the chaperone from

seeing the attractive young Isabella. Then the bandit briefly glanced over his shoulder at the female inside the coach.

'The wolves in these hills like fat, juicy females to eat and I think they will enjoy feasting upon you,' he said before returning his attention to Don Pedro's daughter.

Slowly both Zococa's and the beautiful Isabella's eyes began to adjust to the intense darkness. They could see each other's faint images and neither seemed disappointed.

'Isabella?' the old crone repeated.

'Shut up, you ugly hag,' Zococa said from the corner of his mouth as he pulled the lovely lady toward him. 'You insulted my little elephant and that is unforgivable. One more word and I will stake you out for the wolves to eat.'

Isabella giggled as her over-powering chaperone fell fearfully silent.

'Would you really do that to Maria, Zococa?' she asked.

The bandit winked. '*Sí*, I would do that.'

There was something pure in her eyes. She moved as close as her clothing permitted and felt strangely safe for the first time in her short life.

'My father chose well when he picked you to escort us from the ship to El Sanchez, Zococa,' she sighed as her bosom heaved.

'I agree, dear lady,' the bandit said softly. 'But your companion is most annoying though.'

'I wish to apologise for Maria,' Isabella said softly.

'She should not have spoken so bluntly. I understand the risk you and your Indian friend are taking by escorting us. I am deeply moved by your kindness.'

Zococa tilted his head and smiled widely.

'We expect to be rewarded, pretty lady,' he laughed.

Suddenly she pulled her hands free of his grip and placed them to either side of his face. He stopped grinning as he sensed her face getting closer to his own. Her perfume grew stronger as Isabella pulled his head down toward her.

Zococa was about to speak when her soft lips collided with his own. Zococa was no stranger to the lips of beautiful females but he had never sampled anything like her. She kissed him long and hard for almost a full minute before releasing her grip on his breathless head and returning into the coach. The stunned bandit was in a daze and only recovered when he heard her closing the carriage door behind numerous layers of silk clothing as she re-entered the coach.

'Did that scoundrel kiss you, Isabella?' Maria asked.

'No,' the beautiful Isabella replied. 'I kissed him.'

After tightening the drawstring of his sombrero and clearing his throat, Zococa placed a hand on his saddle horn and raised himself back up on to his pinto stallion. He gathered up his reins and allowed his horse to walk up to the head of the carriage mount. He stopped his horse and looked all around them again.

130

'Where are you, Tahoka?' he whispered as his eyes vainly searched for his trusty companion. 'Why did you ride ahead without telling me what you were doing?'

As the bandit pulled his silver cigar case from his inside breast pocket he could hear something out in the distance. He placed a cigar between his lips and returned the case to his pocket and then struck a match. He filled his lungs with the strong smoke and then heard something ahead of them in the rocks. The dense clouds parted for a few moments and granted the light of the moon to temporarily to illuminate their surroundings.

The coach driver nervously called out to the bandit. Zococa glanced back at the man perched high on the carriage and saw him pointing. Zococa swung back around and then saw a fleeting shadow moving through a gap between two of the largest boulders.

Zococa swiftly dragged his pistol from his holster and cocked its hammer with his thumb as he gripped his reins firmly in his other hand.

'What is it?' the driver frantically asked.

A hollow sound echoed in their ears as the storm clouds once again blanketed the sky in a black cloak. Zococa held his stallion in check as he squinted hard. The sound became clearer to the bandit. It was the noise only hoofs make when crossing rough ground.

Zococa raised his pistol and aimed in the direction he could hear the sound coming from. At least whoever it was could not see them, Zococa thought.

131

The sound continued to intrigue him as he slowly exhaled smoke at his black and white mount's mane. A bead of sweat rolled down his chiselled features from his hatband.

A flash of lightning exploded in the heavens a few miles behind Zococa's back. Its bright light flickered across the entire clearing for a mere heartbeat before allowing the area to return to darkness.

Yet the brief eruption was enough for Zococa to recognize the giant Apache who was steering his gelded grey mount straight towards them.

Zococa shook his head as his heart began to beat normally once more. He lowered his gun as Tahoka eased back on his reins and stopped the horse a few feet from the nose of the pinto stallion.

The smell of burning filled the air as lightning bolts flashed behind them. Zococa watched as the silent Apache warrior dismounted and walked toward him. The eerie flashes of light lit up the mighty Indian as he removed Zococa's canteen from the pinto's saddle horn and took a long drink.

Zococa could see the weariness in the older bandit as Tahoka replaced the stopper and hung the canteen back. The younger bandit could also see the fresh blood that covered Tahoka as he caught his breath and walked back to his grey horse.

The sight of the fresh scalps that hung from Tahoka's beaded belt were gruesome evidence of what the muscular warrior had been up to since he had so swiftly departed. The sky was now alive with rods of deadly forks. It was brighter than day itself

132

and Zococa could see the trail of blood that accompanied the Apache as he reached his horse and mounted.

'You have been busy, little elephant,' Zococa noted as he tapped his spurs against the flanks of the pinto and allowed the stallion to walk up to the side of the grey.

Tahoka raised his head and stared straight at Zococa.

A few gestures with his hands told the younger horseman that he had found and killed every one of the Apache braves that had been lying in wait for them to return through the confines of the rocks.

'All of them?' Zococa checked.

Tahoka gave a violent nod of his head and pointed at the scalps that hung from his belt. The large warrior then turned his horse and waved his hands at the land that lay directly ahead of them and the carriage.

Zococa read the words that the Indian signed. They troubled him even more than the sight of the fresh scalps for they confirmed what he had secretly been dreading since they had set out on this perilous mission. The infamous Don Ricardo was confirming the fears of his brother and had indeed sent out his hired gunmen to prevent the beautiful Isabella from reaching El Sanchez.

The colourful bandit looked back at the carriage knowing that none of its occupants realized the danger they were in.

With lightning flashes dancing across his unusually

drawn features, Zococa leaned closer to Tahoka.

'You have seen many *vaqueros* riding through the canyons, little one?' he asked.

Again, Tahoka nodded and silently described how he had seen more than twenty heavily-armed *vaqueros* heading eastward. That was far more than Zococa had imagined Don Ricardo would be able to muster.

This was not looking good, he thought.

Zococa bit his lower lip. His mind raced as he thought about the beautiful female inside the carriage. He knew that Don Pedro's brother had sent the *vaqueros* to kill the innocent Isabella and were closing in on them.

He looked at the trusty Apache and patted Tahoka on the back as he swung his mount around and signalled the coach driver to start following them again.

Without hesitation, the driver raised and then cracked his long reins across the back of the lathered-up horse between its traces. The carriage jerked into action and started to move toward the horsemen.

Tahoka's hands and fingers spoke to the flamboyant bandit and asked what he intended to do. Zococa sighed heavily and threw his cigar at the sandy ground.

'I intend letting you guide us, Tahoka,' he answered the mute Apache. 'You have seen where the *vaqueros* are. Try and find a safe route out of here.'

Tahoka gave a nod and kicked his gelding hard. The grey was like a bullet leaving the barrel of a six-gun. It sprinted forward with the powerful pinto stallion and black carriage on its heels.

As they entered the depths of the canyon and rode past the lifeless remains of the Apache braves who had been dispatched to their Maker, Zococa kept an eagle eye open for Don Ricardo's deadly henchmen.

Dust kicked up off the hoofs of the horses into the deafening heavens as thunderclaps shook the area. Lightning forks lit up the galloping horses as they thundered along the winding trail.

FIFTEEN

Although Don Ricardo had split his henchmen into two groups and sent them down trails on either side of the land dominated by Apaches, the astute noble-man was only too aware that the cunning Zococa and his native sidekick might be bold enough to risk everything by taking the trail through Indian country.

As Manilla led his ruthless boss and the rest of their deadly force down into a clearing, he raised a hand and stopped his mount. The rest of the riders came to a halt behind the head *vaquero* as the storm grew even angrier above them.

Spots of rain turned into a torrent as the black clouds unleashed their burden. Don Ricardo urged his white charger toward the side of José Manilla's mount.

'Why did you stop here, José?' Don Ricardo snarled as rain drenched the exposed horsemen. 'Explain. I thought we were making good time.'

Manilla turned on his mount and looked from beneath his wide-brimmed hat at the frustrated

Sanchez. He indicated to their left at the smooth boulders set just behind a wall of trees.

'I have travelled this way many times, Don Ricardo,' he explained as he held his soaking wet horse in check. 'The Indians roam this land like fleas on a dog. There is a path through the mighty rocks which leads to the trail that the bandits used to reach Porta Quelbo. It is wide enough for the broadest of horses to navigate.'

Don Ricardo stared through the rain at the rocks where Manilla was pointing. His eyes then darted back at his second in command.

'Are you saying that we should make our way through that narrow trail, José?' he asked his underling. 'But why? Is that not dangerous?'

Manilla moved his horse closer to the white stallion.

'We shall leave half our men here in case the bandits lead your brother's daughter this way,' he said. 'We will reach the Apache trail and lie in wait for the carriage and escort should they survive the Indians.'

Don Ricardo considered the plan carefully and then nodded in agreement.

'You are right, José,' he admitted. 'There is no way that they will be able to reach El Sanchez if we have every trail covered. Whatever route they take, we will be ready to ambush and kill them.'

Five of the horsemen left the others and made their way through the trees before entering the steep-sided gully and cautiously riding along the dark rocks. Water cascaded down the smooth slopes of the boulders to either side of the riders as Don Ricardo led Manilla and the rest of the horsemen through the narrow trail to what was known as the Indian stronghold.

SIXTEEN

The storm was at its zenith. Forceful rain was interspersed by flashes of lethal lightning and ear-splitting thunderclaps. The two horsemen and the following carriage could barely be heard or seen over the skull-numbing noise and blinding light as they travelled along the winding canyon trail.

Tahoka sat astride his grey gelding. His muscular arms rocked back and forth as they physically forced the large animal on through the storm.

They had already passed the bodies of the Indians Tahoka had killed and were getting closer to those he and Zococa had slain hours earlier.

The expressionless warrior seemed unaware of the torrential rain or the storm overhead. His unblinking eyes hid beneath their hooded lids and stared blankly ahead as he led Zococa and the carriage on to their ultimate goal.

Zococa was less consumed.

His quicksilver mind darted from one thought to another as he ensured his pinto stallion kept pace with the gelded mount of his partner.

Thoughts of revenge were never part of the flamboyant bandit's consideration. His thoughts were engulfed by the survival of Isabella and her grumpy chaperone. Nothing more than that would satisfy Zococa.

Yet as always he was fully aware that at any moment the hired gunmen of Don Ricardo might strike out with lethal force and that troubled the youthful bandit.

The razor-sharp senses of Zococa were on high alert as he gripped his reins tightly and rode after the mighty Tahoka. He would require every one of them if he was to get the occupants of the racing carriage out of this desperate plight.

SEVENTEEN

The pair of horsemen led the black coach through the rampaging downpour at pace as lightning splintered across the heavens in search of a fresh target. A tree suddenly exploded ahead of them as one of the electrical rods found its mark. Splinters of burning debris flew in all directions as the riders and speeding carriage passed through the choking smog left in the lightning's wake.

Neither the uncanny Tahoka nor his ever-alert companion slowed the pace of their powerful mounts. They charged along the narrow canyon and then saw the long barrels of a half dozen rifles reflecting the raging overhead lightning.

Don Ricardo and his men had only just cleared the narrow gap between the massive boulders and dismounted when they heard the pounding of horses' hoofs echoing within the confines of the canyon.

'There they are!' Don Ricardo screamed as his *vaqueros* dragged their rifles from the saddle scabbards and cocked them in readiness. 'Kill them!'

José Manilla confirmed his superior's orders with a firm nod of his head. They moved through the driving rain with their lethal weapons firmly gripped in their hands. Within seconds each and every one of the *vaqueros* had aimed their repeating rifles at the approaching riders and coach.

The canyon rocked as their triggers were squeezed. The sound seemed to have no escape from the canyon. It bounced back and forth off the gigantic boulders.

Tahoka had been first to spot the sombrero-wearing gunmen and pulled his six-shooter from its holster as he continued to encourage his grey on. The mighty Apache defied the bullets which cut through the air and whizzed by him.

He blasted back at the bushwhackers.

With red hot tapers of lethal lead snaking through the rainfall toward the startled bandit, Zococa slowed his pinto stallion and put his own body between the carriage and the reckless bullets.

'Keep whipping your horse, *amigo*,' Zococa yelled up at the coach driver as another volley of shots ripped through the air and hit the front of the coach. 'Drive through them.'

Zococa drew his pistol and aimed at the secreted gunmen who hid behind a cloud of lingering gunsmoke. He squeezed its trigger over and over again.

As bullets flew back and forth between the two sides, the bandit caught a glimpse of two of the riflemen falling. Then he heard Tahoka grunt. His eyes darted to the Apache.

142

It was obvious that the muscular Indian had been hit. Tahoka rocked and grabbed hold of his mount's mane to prevent himself from falling off his saddle.

As Zococa spurred his pinto, he saw Tahoka drag his hefty hatchet from his belt and throw it with all his force at the line of bushwhackers. The steel blade sunk into the chest of José Manilla and did not stop travelling until it collided with the vaquero's backbone.

With blood pouring from his hideous wound, Manilla gave out a sickening scream and fell between Don Ricardo and the last of his remaining hired men as the wounded Apache rode past them. Don Ricardo went to cock his rifle again when he was knocked off his feet by Zococa's leaping pinto.

Before the rest of the *vaqueros* had time to organize themselves, the black carriage was driven straight through them. They went flying as Zococa turned his stallion and sent the last of his bullets into them.

The bandit hauled his long leathers hard to his right and chased his companions at full speed. Hoof dust mingled into the acrid gunsmoke as the small band headed on the last leg to El Sanchez.

With every stride of his pinto's long legs, Zococa thought about the noise he had heard from Tahoka. He had heard the Apache make chilling sounds before, but nothing like the guttural sound he had made when the *vaqueros'* shots hit him. As a terrifying dread overwhelmed Zococa, the bandit spurred harder.

The mighty stallion powered its way after his

master's colleagues as bullets carved through the darkness from the *vaqueros*' rifles. There was an urgency in the pounding heart of the intrepid bandit.

Tahoka had always been courageous.

Zococa feared that the giant Apache warrior might have also become foolhardy and ridden straight at the devilish rifle fire without considering the bloody consequences.

EIGHTEEN

Don Ricardo turned over and stared at the hideous sight of the dead men who lay beside him. After prodding the lifeless body of Manilla a few times, he reluctantly accepted the fact that his right hand man was dead. The nobleman had never seen death close up before and it chilled him to the bone. As lightning flashed above the place where they had fallen, he realized that time was quickly running out if he were to ever stop his niece from reaching the sanctuary of El Sanchez.

Fury erupted inside his chest. He scrambled back to his feet, snatched his still-smoking rifle off the churned up ground and stared down at the dead *vaqueros*. Then he spotted that two of their number, closest to the canyon wall, were unhurt.

Don Ricardo dusted himself off and screamed at the dazed hired gunmen.

'Get our horses,' he fumed as he quickly reloaded the magazine of his rifle. 'We are going after them.'

The pair of men led their mounts out into the canyon and watched as Don Ricardo angrily mounted the white stallion and gathered up his long leathers. Neither of them relished encountering Zococa or his Apache friend for a second time, but knew that the single-minded nobleman had only one thought filling his mind.

Don Ricardo was hell-bent on killing his brother's daughter before she reached the secure arms of her father. Even the driving rain could not cool the fire which blazed in his heartless soul.

'We will never catch up with them, *señor*,' said one of the *vaqueros*, known simply as Ramón, as he and the other surviving gunman clambered on top of their bedraggled mounts. 'They have too much lead.'

Don Ricardo levelled his repeating rifle on his men and cocked its trigger.

'We will catch them, Ramón,' he spat. 'Pray that we catch and kill them. For if we do not, I shall kill you.'

Both the *vaqueros* nodded. They understood the deranged mind of their paymaster only too well. They knew that the ambitious sibling of Don Pedro would never tolerate anything else but the killing of his niece and her protectors.

A cruel grin carved across the wet face of Don Ricardo as he swung his large horse around and then drove his spurs deep into the flanks of the white stallion.

The three riders galloped away from their dead comrades and after the coach and its escorts. As far as the insane nobleman was concerned, there could only be one outcome. He would be one step closer to becoming the ruler of the mysterious El Sanchez.

*

Zococa's powerful pinto stallion had charged through the driving rain for miles before he saw the tail of the black carriage ahead of him. As he neared, he caught sight of the lumbering Tahoka still leading them.

Yet the sight of the Apache did not settle Zococa's concerns as he rode past the body of the coach and neared his friend's broad back.

Only stubbornness was keeping the warrior on the back of the gelded grey. The closer Zococa got to the Indian, the more he noticed that Tahoka was slumped over the neck of his horse's mane.

Zococa reached out and touched his bedraggled friend.

'Tahoka?' he shouted above the thunderous din, but there was no hint of any reaction in the wounded Apache. 'You cannot die, my little one. Who would scold the great Zococa?'

The young bandit grabbed the grey mount's bridle and pulled it back until the horse responded and stopped. Within a few seconds the large Tahoka toppled toward the awaiting arms of Zococa who then eased the Apache's fall to the ground.

As Zococa knelt beside the prostrate Apache between their two horses, the carriage forced its way through the blinding rainfall and was halted beside the bandit.

'Give me a hand, *amigo*,' Zococa called through the rain to the coach driver who hastily descended and moved through the muddy ground to the side of the troubled bandit.

'What do you want me to do, Zococa?'

'Help me lift him,' Zococa replied as he slid his hands under the giant Apache's armpits. 'We must put my friend into the coach with the women.'

The startled carriage driver looked through the waterfall that flowed from the wide brim of his hat. He hesitantly touched the soaking wet jacket of the bandit. Their eyes met.

'He seems dead, Zococa.'

'Grab his legs,' Zococa said firmly.

Both men strained, took the warrior's weight between them and then lifted Tahoka off the ground and turned. They staggered to the carriage just as Isabella opened the vehicle's nearest door.

As the females made room and Tahoka's unconscious body was gently eased on to the seat opposite, both the driver and Zococa heard something behind them battling through the storm.

'What is that noise, Zococa?' Isabella asked as the bandit gently closed the carriage door and the driver scrambled up the side of the coach back to his seat.

'I fear it is the men who tried to ambush us back in the canyon, little lady,' Zococa answered as the sound of pounding horse hoofs grew ever louder as Don Ricardo and his two *vaqueros* chased their elusive prey.

Isabella touched the bandit's fingers as they rested on the vehicle's door. A brilliant flash of lightning lit up the faces of both the heiress and her escort for a brief moment.

'We shall look after your friend, Zococa,' she purred seductively. 'He has paid dearly for looking after a total stranger. I am forever in the debt of both of you.'

Isabella pulled herself back into the vehicle.

Even the darkness of the carriage interior could not hide the sight of the wounded Tahoka from the concerned bandit's eyes. He reached inside the carriage. His fingertips touched the beautiful female's lips before he turned on his heels, took two steps and leapt on to his ornate saddle and grabbed his reins.

'Follow me, *amigo*,' Zococa told the driver, hauled the stallion around and spurred hard. The pinto galloped forward into the mist which rose from the sodden ground.

The coach feverishly trailed the huge horse into the darkness as Zococa strained his eyes and studied the soft muddy ground as he valiantly tried to retrace their tracks from hours earlier.

Zococa pulled back on his reins and halted his pinto abruptly. He realized that the horsemen who chased them were getting closer with every beat of his pounding heart but there was nothing he could do to prevent it.

Don Ricardo was catching up with the carriage as it laboured through the muddy terrain. Zococa knew that there were few horses who could have caught up with his black and white stallion when it was given free rein, but he had been forced to slow his mount's pace because of the carriage and its precious cargo.

After a few moments, the coach caught up with

him and Zococa watched as it carried on the slippery trail that led to the treacherous route which snaked through the quicksand.

Zococa looked at the heavens.

The rain had stopped and the black clouds had drifted further west to reveal the moon. The worst of the storm was over, but Zococa knew that a far worse one was approaching from behind them.

He removed his silver cigar case from his breast pocket and plucked a slim cigar from within it. He snapped the case shut and returned it before finding a box of matches from deep inside his pants. He extracted a dry match and ran his thumbnail across its coloured tip.

As a flame erupted in his cupped palms he spotted Tahoka's gelded grey horse trotting through the gloom behind him. The horse continued on after the carriage as Zococa sucked in the cigar flame and filled his lungs with strong smoke.

Zococa shook the match and tossed the blackened wood at the mud. He then pulled the cigar free of his lips and stared into the darkness.

The unruly ground had slowed their deadly pursuers just as it had slowed the carriage. Zococa filled his lungs again and then propelled the cigar far away from where he sat atop his stallion.

As the cigar hit the seemingly firm ground, it sank.

The quicksand stretched further away from the place where he had assumed it ended. With smoke drifting through his clenched teeth, Zococa became suddenly concerned.

His eyes darted back to where he had last seen the black carriage disappear from view. The driver did not know it, but the land he was driving his coach into was littered with deadly patches of quicksand.

Zococa hauled his long leathers to his right and spurred.

The pinto stallion was about to respond to the razor sharp spurs when suddenly Zococa's attention was drawn to his left and the winding trail they had just travelled along. To his horror, Zococa watched as the three horsemen forced their bedraggled mounts through the mist.

The bandit held the pinto in check for a few moments. Then the moon betrayed him.

'There!' Don Ricardo and his pair of hired henchmen pulled their rifles from their saddle scabbards and started blasting at the startled Zococa.

Red hot tapers of potential death flew through the air and zeroed in on the horseman. After steadying the stallion, Zococa hung low and pressed his head against the neck of the horse as his spurs frantically jabbed the horse's flanks.

Zococa steered his horse between the lethal volley of bullets and headed after the carriage. His mind desperately searched for a plan but the only one which surfaced was the one which yelled for him to stay alive.

NINETEEN

There were few horsemen as skilled as Zococa but even he was having trouble keeping the muscular stallion upright on the muddy road. It took every last scrap of the bandit's strength to prevent the pinto from collapsing as its hoofs slid on the slimy surface. The rain might have ceased its torrential downpour but the evidence of the previous hour's storm was everywhere.

Zococa glanced over his shoulder as the fiery mount reached a moonlit ridge. He dragged back on his long leathers and stared back at his pursuers and watched as they fired their repeating rifles. A trio of plumes encircled the barrels of their weaponry before Zococa heard the shots. Luckily for the exhausted bandit, the treacherous ground hampered their ability to aim just as it dogged his ability to get his mount galloping.

Bullets flew over his sombrero like lost hornets vainly seeking their nest. Zococa desperately turned and looked ahead once more and squinted through the half-light in search of the black carriage.

Then he saw the glint of moonlight far below the ridge as it glanced across the side of the labouring vehicle. Zococa's heart sank as he watched the coach stagger to a boggy halt on a bend.

'Damn it,' Zococa cursed before jabbing his spurs into the stallion. 'Do not get stuck there.'

The large black and white horse obeyed its master's spurs and somehow navigated a route down the ridge and on to the flat terrain. As Zococa managed to keep his mount upright he heard more shots behind him.

As he urged the horse on toward the carriage he knew that the three horsemen were still beyond the ridge. He knew that none of their shots could hit him until they cleared the high ridge.

As he reached the coach he noted that its wheels were well and truly stuck in the soft ground. The driver looked helpless and did not know what to do.

For a moment, neither did Zococa.

'The horse is exhausted, Zococa,' the driver stated fearfully as more shots rang out beyond the moonlit rise behind them. 'She cannot pull the carriage out of this bog.'

Zococa removed his saddle rope from his saddle horn and hastily uncoiled it. He then looped it over the closest wheel and tightened its knot before wrapping the tail of the rope around the ornate horn of his saddle. Then he moved ahead of the carriage and forced the pinto stallion to take the strain of the taut rope.

The powerful stallion was at least three hands taller than the carriage horse and much stronger. Zococa lashed the shoulders of the pinto with the loose tails of his reins and gradually sensed movement. It did not take long before the bandit noticed the wheels start rotating as the vehicle escaped the mire.

When the coach was clear of the deep mud, Zococa tossed the rope on to the roof of the passing carriage and glanced into its interior. Tahoka was still motionless opposite the two very different females.

'How far is it to El Sanchez, Zococa?' Isabella asked as her hands gripped the open window of the door.

Zococa did not have time to reply. Suddenly three more shots rang out across the moonlit area. He dragged his reins up to his chest and looked over his shoulder at the trio of horsemen appeared on the ridge crest.

Without a second thought, Zococa looked up at the coach driver and pointed at the winding trail.

'Head between the trees, *amigo*,' the bandit instructed the terrified driver. 'Whatever you do, do not stray to either side even if the ground looks firmer. Believe me, it is not.'

The driver looked puzzled as he lifted his whip and coiled the carriage reins around his right wrist.

'I do not understand, Zococa,' he exclaimed. 'Why do I have to stay on the trail between those trees? That looks very muddy ground to me.'

Zococa pointed at the small man.

'There is deadly quicksand to both sides of that trail, *amigo*,' he insisted. 'If you venture on to it, you shall all die in a most horrible way. Savvy?'

The fearful man nodded and then cracked his whip above his head. The horse between the traces responded and began to head to where the bandit had indicated.

The *vaqueros* had been quiet for a few moments as they rested their horses on the ridge. They had taken the opportunity to reload their weapons' magazines as they studied the moonlit scene below their high vantage point.

Zococa's eyes darted between the rocking carriage and the ridge as he swiftly checked his silver pistol. The six-shooter was loaded with the last of his ammunition as he swung the stallion to face the horsemen.

The bandit realized that they were out of range of his .45 but knew the riflemen could easily hit him with their long-barrelled carbines. Despite this chilling fact, Zococa squared up to the three men who sat with their rifle stocks on their thighs.

Ominously, the riders began to negotiate the steep slope down to where the flamboyant bandit awaited. Beads of sweat defied the cool evening temperature and trailed down his face as his unblinking eyes watched Don Ricardo and his pair of *vaqueros* steadily close the distance between them.

Had Zococa even suspected that one of the three riders was the ringleader Don Ricardo himself, the bandit might have reacted differently, but to him they were all just ambushers bathed in the cloak of night.

As they drew ever closer, a million fleeting thoughts flashed through Zococa's mind. He attempted to think of a way that he could stop them before they prevented the attractive Isabella from reaching the sanctuary of her father's land. The trouble was they had him outgunned and this time surprise was no longer an option.

'Think, you handsome fool,' Zococa told himself as his index finger curled around the trigger of his pistol. 'Think of something while you still have no bullet holes in your body.'

Suddenly, the three horsemen lowered the barrels of their rifles and charged. Within a mere heartbeat, the night air was illuminated by a barrage of white hot gunsmoke.

FINALE

The riders soon discovered that it was virtually impossible to operate their Winchesters' mechanisms, aim and fire and also keep control of weary horses who were nearly knee-deep in the rain sodden ground beneath their hoofs. Each of the horses slid as their masters attempted to remain on their saddles as they descended from the ridge.

Zococa could not believe his good fortune as he watched the horsemen's plight. To the bandit they looked as though they were all drunk as his thumb dragged back his gun hammer.

Shots passed within inches of the defiant bandit as he carefully took aim and fired. The *vaquero* to the right was hit dead centre and rolled over his saddle cantle before crashing into the muddy slope behind his mount's hoofs.

Then a bullet tore his sombrero off his black hair. The drawstring snapped and sent the wide-brimmed hat swirling backward. Zococa did not flinch or move as he cocked the pistol again and fired at the *vaquero* known as Ramón.

Again his shot was true.

Ramón buckled as the deadly accurate shot went straight through him. The lifeless *vaquero* dropped his rifle as the horse fell forward in the mud. The animal was trapped in the unforgiving mire but his master was more than a little dead.

Somehow to Zococa's surprise, Don Ricardo managed to keep his white charger upright. Then he brutally spurred the wide-eyed horse and forced it to scramble over Ramón's fallen mount. The nobleman steadied the white horse and then thrust his spurs into its flanks again.

The horse leapt like a steeplechaser.

It cleared the muddy slope and landed on the flat ground forty feet from where the bandit sat astride his pinto. Zococa watched as the nobleman cranked the hand guard of his rifle and brought the lethal firearm up to his shoulder.

Zococa swung his pinto around and began chasing the black carriage as it cleared the deadly ground and disappeared from view in the trees.

The expert rider heard the rifle shot behind him and felt the hot bullet graze his ribs. With gritted teeth, he steered the pinto stallion between the trees and followed the distinctive tracks left by the coach.

Zococa then hauled back on his long leathers and stopped his horse's progress abruptly. The bandit then dismounted and watched as Don Ricardo rode his white charger straight at him.

The wounded bandit was about to fire his pistol

when he realized that the elegant rider was not following him on the safe trail. Instead Don Ricardo was riding directly across the seemingly solid ground with his rifle clutched in one hand as his other fist firmly gripped his reins.

The white stallion had only taken three long strides when it began to vanish into the quicksand. As his magnificent horse disappeared from beneath him, the nobleman began to thrash at the unstable ground.

Zococa held his reins and stepped toward the terrified man and touched his brow.

'It is quicksand, *amigo*,' he informed.

'Help me, peasant!' Don Ricardo screamed out as he sank deeper into the ravenous sand. 'I am Don Ricardo Sanchez. I will make you a rich man if you save my life. Don't just stand there, do something!'

'Sorry, *amigo*. I work for another Sanchez.' Zococa shrugged and then holstered his pistol. He remained beside the pinto until Don Ricardo had slipped into the bottomless pit of quicksand. He then turned, grabbed his saddle horn and mounted his black and white stallion.

Suddenly the sound of awakening birds filled the air as the first rays of a new day lavished their glory on the beautiful yet deadly area.

'Come on, horse,' Zococa winced as he touched the bloody graze on his side. 'The pretty lady is safely in her father's land by now. If we ride fast I might catch up to the beautiful little lady before she reaches Don Pedro. Her lips were so soft and I am sure she will be very grateful for my valour.'

Zococa looked down at the green quicksand. There was no hint of what had just occurred a few moments earlier. As he jerked his reins and got the pinto moving again after the fleeing carriage, Zococa thought about his trusty friend.

'I hope my little elephant is still alive, horse,' he sighed as they entered the trees and followed the tracks left by the fleeing carriage. 'It would take a lot of digging to make a hole big enough for Tahoka to fit in. Besides, I am very tired.'